Letting

First Edition

Copyright © Brooke Powley 2014

Brooke Powley asserts the moral right to be identified as the author of this work.

All rights reserved. No part of this publication may be reproduced, stored in a retrieval system, or transmitted, in any form or by any means, electronic, mechanical, photocopying, recording, or otherwise, without prior permission.

Except for those in the public domain, all the characters in this book are fictitious and resemblance to actual persons, living or dead, is purely coincidental.

www.brookepowley.com

Acknowledgements

I promised myself that I would never be one of those authors who wrote long and rambling acknowledgement pages, but this time there are just too many people to thank, so apologies in advance...

To Pete, who has to put up with the agonising over plot developments, characters, formatting, editing, book covers etc over dinner, in the car, up a mountain... you might get a bit of peace for a while now!

To Ava, who has had to fight for her computer time when I'm having a book blitz and is then watched like a hawk because she cannot be trusted not to delete important files by accident (thank goodness for external hard drives!)

To my family and friends - who have been there for me over the years through the bad times and the good.

Special thanks as always to my beady-eyed proofreading team; Katie Wright, Wayne McClellan, Faye Cooke, Clare Oatham-Vital and Anne Mathieson.

Lastly, thank you to my readers. Your positive words have encouraged me to hurry up and write book two – I hope it lives up to your expectations!

To Ava

Chapter One

The accident happened on a Sunday evening in early December. The weather was cold and there was a slight dusting of snow on the ground. It made the village look like a picture postcard – snow clung helplessly to tree branches, and people wandered around in winter knitwear, with rosy red cheeks, as if they had nowhere to be and nowhere to go.

There were three weeks left until Christmas. The Parker family had put the tree up early, as they did every year. The children were caught up in the excitement of it all - Finn constantly singing 'Jingle Bells', Millie's eyes glistening at all the twinkling lights, and only Poppy had seemed to muster enough self-restraint not to open the entire chocolate advent calendar the moment her parents backs were turned.

Emma Parker was always organised in the run up for Christmas, which surprised her husband, James. The children's main presents had been put safely in the loft, weeks before; the Christmas cards had been long since sent out to various family and friends across the country, and each card that had landed through the letterbox to Rose Cottage had been ticked-off on a grand master list. *Three strikes and you're out* Emma would say to James while mulling over the Christmas card list, and he would tease her about it every year.

Emma had never sent out any cards until James had moved into Rose Cottage. Christmas didn't even appear on her radar, and why would it?

Her parents were Jehovah's Witnesses. Christmas presents were not a part of Emma's childhood.

The Parker family were having a quiet weekend - nothing out of the ordinary. They took the children to the garden centre on the other side of the village, to look at all of the Christmas paraphernalia. It was a trove of festivities for children, though the Christmas section seemed to appear earlier and earlier with each passing year.

In the afternoon, they walked the short distance from their house to Rydal caves, ignoring the 'do not enter' sign and letting the children splash through the water in their wellingtons and watching them as they wandered towards the back of the dark cave – all the time looking out for Gruffalo clues which was Finn and Poppy's new obsession. On the way back home, they indulged in hot chocolates in the deserted tearoom, before letting the children cross the stepping-stones with excitement - as if they had never seen them before in their lives.

On Sunday morning, Emma and James took the children to the only indoor play area in the village, Rufty Tufty's, which was owned by a local family that they knew to say hello to. James liked to have a chance to read the papers, while Emma read on her kindle, and they managed to drink their coffees and unwind a little in relative peace as the children let off some steam. Even Millie was good at making herself busy in the baby area, sometimes daring to join the others if there weren't too many children running around like wild animals let out of a zoo.

In the afternoon, James's parents, Meg and Eric popped round briefly. They arrived armed with various children's books and bags of chocolate buttons. '*They were on offer*' James's Mum told him in a half apology, as she handed them out to her flock of greedy little grandchildren.

Since the children had been small, James had always made a point of trying not to work at the weekends. Not just because he didn't want to be remembered as an absent father, but also because he didn't want all the paperwork to take over his life, because it easily could if he let it.

Life was different for Emma. She was with the children every night of the week, every school reading book that they brought home, every swimming lesson and all those nights that James worked late and missed bath time. She never complained, but James knew that it must have been difficult for her. All those hours in the house by herself, like a prisoner. Sunday nights were her chance to be free. Her chance to catch up with her friend, Hannah, over a drink, without the constraints that came with taking a gaggle of children with you everywhere you went.

James barely said goodbye to his wife as she left the house that evening, and it was one of the things that he would later regret. Emma was wearing jeans and her winter coat - fastened up right to the top.

Emma and Hannah had been friends ever since they were little girls, when Emma had moved to Ambleside with her parents and sister. They had both grown up in the same part of the village, and had stayed in touch when Emma moved away to Manchester to finish her nurses training. Hannah was different from Emma's other close friend, Beth, who Emma had met at the toddler group which ran in the village hall once a week. The toddler group offered a chance for parents to drink copious amounts of tea and talk about who really had the worst night's sleep, which baby had the highest raging temperature, and which toddler was experiencing the worst of the 'terrible twos'.

Though Emma and Beth seemed to have much more in common these days, James always thought that Hannah gave Emma a good escape route to her old life. Hannah's long-term partner, Jim, worked away on the oilrigs, mostly, they thought, because the money was good, but it left Hannah on her own a lot of the time. Hannah and Jim didn't have children, and the Parkers often wondered why. Most Sundays, Emma wandered over to Hannah's house in the early evening because it was easier for her to pop out when James was home, than to arrange and pay for a babysitter when he wasn't. A night out was suddenly expensive if you had to add babysitters to your evening.

James went outside to the garden and shut the hens in. Emma had bought the hens when Poppy was small, shortly before he had sold his house in Kendal and moved in. At last count, they had five hens of various breeds, though James thought the flock seemed to chop and change as often as the children needed new shoes, and sometimes it was hard for him to keep track. The children just loved chasing them around the garden, checking for eggs and throwing out handfuls of corn. But all five hens were off-lay now for the winter, except for one of the oldest, March, who seemed to be the only hen that was not put-off by the abysmal Lake District weather, which was well-known for taking no prisoners.

Back inside the house, James poured himself a glass of red wine, and sat down on the sofa with some papers that needed marking. He worked fulltime at the University in Lancaster, which was about forty-five minutes from their home in Ambleside, the Lake District. James had managed to secure a job there after completing his MA and working for a couple of years as a lecturer in Manchester. When he had taken the job in Lancaster, he had moved back to Kendal so that he could be more help to his ageing parents.

Before Emma, James had travelled from his old house in Kendal to his job in Lancaster every day, but he preferred the quiet life in Ambleside, where they lived just outside of the village centre but close enough to be able to walk in for a loaf of bread or a paper. James liked his job; he didn't mind the travelling too much – it gave him a chance to listen to the radio in peace, if nothing else. The holiday leave was better than most companies – long summers where they could pack up the car and the rabble, and head off to France for a few weeks of glorious sunshine. Okay, so he had to go on a few residential trips a year, and had to take groups out in all weathers, which was often grim, especially if the weather was bad. No job is perfect though, is it? That's what James often thought to himself – you could always find something to complain about if you tried hard enough.

After a couple of hours of marking, James put his papers back on his desk and glanced at his watch. It was gone eleven o'clock. It was unusual for Emma to stay out this late. But he didn't give it much more than a passing thought as he checked on the children and climbed into their bed. No doubt, she would turn up with some tale about Hannah's latest exploits. Hannah, for a woman in her early-thirties, did seem to get herself into some muddles. He knew Emma would be complaining about her lack of sleep in the morning as she poured herself an extra coffee before going to wake the children. Lack of sleep was one thing that Emma didn't do well on.

James slept lighter than he normally would have that night. He was in full-parent mode, listening for any movements or whimpers since he knew that he was the only responsible adult in the house. When he woke at just after 4 am, Emma still wasn't home.

Five, six, and still nothing.

James eventually got up at six-thirty and jumped in the shower. Then he let out the hens who completely ignored the opening of the henhouse door, as the weather was dark and grim. Later, when the sun had risen, they would have their usual morning fight over the corn that James had scattered across the pathway.

Usually, James left for work at just after seven-thirty – he always thought that it was better to beat the traffic, as it gave him time to grab a coffee and sit in his office for a while before the madness of the working day began.

Finn woke first, confused by the lack of his mother, followed closely by Poppy. James threw some weetabix into two bowls before bracing himself for Millie, who was not a happy bunny if she had to be woken up in the mornings

Funny isn't it, how children can be so unalike, in looks and personality? Finn was very fair with blonde, wavy hair, while the girls' hair was darker, a softer shade of brown, and their skin more prone to tanning in the sun. Finn was more happy-go-lucky than his sisters, who could both be serious and demanding. There was no logic or reason for it and the Parkers were happy with their family, even if people did look twice, especially when they were on holiday, as one of them called for Finn to come and join his two darker sisters.

Seven-thirty came and went.

Eight o'clock.

Eight-fifteen.

James was starting to become annoyed, agitated, at the lack of his wife. *Where was she?* He dressed the children as quickly as he could, made the packed lunches, and called his mother to inform her that he would be dropping off Millie on his way to work because usually Emma didn't work on Mondays and Millie usually stayed at home with her.

It was all a hassle that James could do without, especially first thing on this Monday morning, as his manager was coming into his department in the afternoon. He had a tonne of things to organise and sort out before his manager would make his appearance. To make matters worse, he was now running an hour late, which meant that he had an extra hour to make up at the end of his working day, which was always a killer in the long, dark winter nights.

The journey would take him twice as long now, as he would be passing Kendal at the worst time ever – the time when all the other workers were heading into town and all the secondary school children, from the outlying villages, were trying to get to school.

Every time James tried phoning Emma's mobile, it kept going straight to voicemail, which again seemed strange. Emma was well known for having her iphone on her at all times; she used it as her organiser – her calendar, shopping list, and to check her emails. James would always catch her tapping away on it at night when she was supposed to be relaxing, as if people couldn't wait until morning.

In a last ditch attempt to find out what was going on James picked up the phone and called Hannah. James had put it off because he didn't like to be that kind of husband – the kind that had to check up on his wife. But this was a near emergency. He didn't have time for this - Emma should have been home hours ago. He needed to know what was going on, where she was, and when she would be coming home.

"She left at ten-fifteen last night, James," Hannah replied to him, calmly.

James barely had time to process what Hannah was saying to him when he noticed that Poppy had opened the front door to two uniformed policemen, their faces white and ashen.

He threw the phone down on the coffee table and walked towards the front door.

"Mr. James Parker?" the taller of the two officers asked.

"Yes?" he replied.

"I wonder if we could come in and have a word with you," he said, eyeing Poppy and Finn who were now both stood staring at the police officers in the doorway.

"In private?" the other, shorter officer added.

James nodded his head, gave the children a couple of biscuits, and told them to take Millie and go to play upstairs for five minutes while he talked to the policemen. The three adults listened as the little thuds headed up the stairs and the bedroom door closed behind them, before the smaller officer began to speak.

"I'm afraid we come bearing bad news, Mr. Parker..." he said.

Time stood still.

James Parker's whole world collapsed.

Chapter Two

There are times when you can pinpoint an event that changed your life. That something might be big – the birth of a child, a wedding, a trip to Australia. But sometimes something may seem so insignificantly small it doesn't even register on your radar in your day-to-day life but it will inevitably set off a chain of events that could be irreversible.

Driving to the hospital in a haze of thoughts, James Parker was thinking about the first time he met Emma - the way that her soft blonde hair fell across her face, the way her blue eyes looked at him intensely, the way she walked around the supermarket with Poppy as if she had nowhere else to be and nowhere else to go. He watched them from a distance, as he was filling up his own trolley with the usual weekly food shopping – bags of pasta, milk, chicken, and cheese.

Poppy had thrown her soft, brown bear out of her seat in the trolley while Emma was looking the other way at the yogurts when it happened. James was the person who picked up the bear and handed it back. Sometime later - in the supermarket cafe, when there were no seats left, Emma and Poppy came and sat next to him. The rest, as they say, is history.

James often wondered how his life would have been if he hadn't gone shopping to Asda on that particular Friday afternoon - if he had never met Emma. He tried not to dwell on it too much, because he didn't want to think about how his life had been before – the long, lonely nights by himself, the constant jibes from his parents about finding a woman, and watching all of his other friends grow up and have families of their own. One by one, his friends and colleagues didn't have time to meet up with him on a Saturday night for a beer in the pub – the children were teething, or had a football match early next morning, the wife wanted to go out, or the dog was sick. For James, the years became longer and sadder. Finding Emma had been a breath of fresh air, made his life have an exciting edge to it. The day that they met must have been fate. Or, at least, that's what James liked to believe.

The policeman told James, in the stunned silence of his own kitchen, that the milkman had found Emma's body on the side of the road, at just gone four am that morning. Her head was battered and her blood seeped from her lifeless body onto the road in which she lay. The milkman had discovered only a faint pulse and called 999 immediately. Police and an ambulance were dispatched, and arrived on the scene within minutes. The paramedics decided that the extent of Emma's injuries meant an air ambulance was the best thing for her. Her head trauma was classed as severe and it was likely that she could have been in the unconscious state for more than six hours. The hospital in Preston was well known for dealing with more complex cases. Even though her injuries were serious, she was in a 'stable' condition – heavily sedated while they were doing all they could to find out exactly what was wrong with her. Not getting any better, but equally not getting any worse.

James couldn't remember everything that the police officers had said to him that morning, because it had all happened so quickly; he could barely process new information as his brain struggled to cope with what it had already been told. He nodded glumly until the police left him alone with the children.

Somehow, James managed to drop off the oldest two children at school without having to engage in conversation with any of the other parents. It's not what they want to hear at the school gates, is it? *Too close to home*, James thought to himself silently. They don't want bad things to happen to people they know because, inevitably, it could mean that bad things might happen to them. It was a foolish way of thinking, but they would still think it, nonetheless. *They would find out about it soon enough*, James thought as he returned to his car. It was one of the downsides to living in a village – bad news travelled fast.

Millie was in the car with James during the drive down to Preston hospital, jabbering away to herself, playing with one of those annoying vtech toys she had probably been given for her birthday. She was oblivious to the fact that her safe little world was in jeopardy. James told her that her Mummy was sick, but she barely batted an eyelid as he strapped her back into the car, which he had parked in the churchyard next to the school. *But then, why would she?* James thought. *How could she possibly begin to understand?* James called his parents and asked them to come as soon as they could – Millie needed someone to look after her, someone to keep her world normal. He told them that he didn't know yet - how bad Emma really was or what would happen next.

He parked the car in the hospital car park; he didn't have any change for the car park, so it was left without a ticket. He'd deal with that later, he thought, as he strapped Millie into the pushchair that was in the car boot, and ran at full speed towards the hospital reception desk.

"Emma Parker," he said to the woman, offering no explanation as to who she was, or which part of the hospital he thought she might be in. The receptionist didn't seem phased and called for a nurse to show him the way to the intensive care unit, which was down - what seemed to James - like a giant maze of corridors.

Another nurse, who was sitting at the reception desk at the ICU, greeted him with a warm smile. She began giving James a briefing of what had happened to Emma since she had arrived in the air ambulance, and he struggled to keep up with it all. The nurse looked down towards Millie,

"I'm afraid we don't allow children under three in the Intensive Care Unit, unless there is an exceptional circumstance, but you can leave her here and I'll keep a good eye on her for you...," she said kindly.

It hadn't even crossed his mind that Millie wouldn't be allowed inside. His instinct had been to get straight to Preston as soon as he could, which didn't mean allowing extra time for the detour round Windermere to drop her off with his parents,

17

or worse a detour round Kendal to drop her off with the in-laws.

He looked down at Millie, who was now chewing on the corner of her buggy book – 'The Very Hungry Caterpillar'. In a different time, Emma and James would have laughed at this moment. Millie was such a glutton. It was the only thing that made her unlike her other two siblings, who were both picky, fussy eaters.

"My parents are on their way; they shouldn't be long," he managed to utter.

James waved goodbye to Millie, who luckily had never been a clingy child and was happy being left with anyone at anytime, and he followed a doctor to Emma's bed.

The first thing he really noticed was the smell of strong disinfectant, mixed with the smell of alcohol antibacterial hand gel, which was located at the foot of every bed. The second thing, as they drew nearer, was the noise of all the hospital equipment – the soft bleeping of machines and the whir of the ventilator. James half-wondered, *how do they expect people to get any rest with all that noise going on?*

Then he saw her.

Emma was lying in the bed, wires coming out of her in all directions. She was covered in various scrapes and bandages. James noticed that her left arm was in a cast, that there was dried blood covering a lot of her hair. It was strange, James thought, because his wife almost looked peaceful, at rest. Without all the equipment, he could have easily been looking at Emma on any night of the week, apart from the fact that she rarely slept on her back, that she wriggled around in her sleep so much that the duvet usually ended up upside down and back to front.

"Oh Emma," he said, taking her hand, gently stroking her hair. James watched her chest rise and fall. He listened to the steady beat of her heart on the monitor. She was still here, with them. That was the main thing, for now. They would work the rest out, wouldn't they? Face whatever challenges lay ahead? James thought that one day, he and Emma would look back on this moment and laugh, as if the frightening reality of now wasn't really happening, as if someone could wave a magic wand and everything would just go back to normal. Things would get better; they had to, didn't they? He just had to believe it.

Chapter Three

What can you say, in all honesty, about a day that destroyed your life?

That first day, the day of the accident, James wanted answers. He wanted someone to be accountable, responsible. He was angry and irrational. The fact that they *didn't know* what had happened to his wife just wasn't good enough. Why weren't they out there, looking for who had done this to her? Scouring every house in every street until they found them?

Emma lay oblivious to the chaos that was unfolding around her. They sent her for a brain scan, an MRI. James somehow tried to keep it all together, tried not to fall apart in front of his parents, his children. Things were bad enough as they were, he thought.

It soon became clear that Emma wouldn't be going anywhere, anytime soon. They sent a consultant, Mr. Abraham, to talk to James and he couldn't bring himself to ask that question – would Emma ever fully recover? - just *yet*. James couldn't face the truth - that his perfect, wonderful wife might never wake up from this nightmare that they suddenly found themselves in. That his children might grow up without a mother. That was the reality that James might have to face, but he was not ready to give it more than a passing thought. Not yet.

The nurse had given him a large pile of forms to fill out and Mr. Abraham wanted to talk about them, talk to James about what was going to happen to Emma next.

"Unfortunately, Mr. Parker, your wife lost a lot of blood in the air ambulance..." he began, letting his voice trail off. James knew where this was going. He knew what Mr. Abraham was going to say, what he was going to ask him.

"We have refrained, so far, from giving Emma a blood transfusion because of the medical codicil that we found in her NHS records during her admission. As her next of kin, Mr. Parker, we need to know how you want us to proceed. It's fortunate that we found out who she was in time, because she wasn't carrying her medical documents..." Mr. Abraham allowed his voice trailed off again.

James looked directly at the consultant, straight into his eyes. Mr. Abraham wasn't giving anything away; he wasn't demanding or trying to persuade him that Emma should be given pints of blood immediately. James had worried about this 'catch twenty-two' situation for many years. He had hoped that it would never come to this.

James thought about Emma's parents, about what they would think knowing their daughter had been the recipient of blood. Maybe he was being selfish by thinking that Emma wasn't *much* of a Witness these days. How could she be, buying all those presents for Christmases and birthdays? She could have left it all to him, like he had suggested the first year that Christmas had come around. But she didn't; she insisted on helping, insisted that it shouldn't be up to him to do it all by himself. James knew that she rarely stepped foot in the Kingdom

Hall anymore, that she was no longer a regular at the Sunday meetings. That Emma liked her steaks cooked *medium-rare* for goodness sake, all that sacred blood dripping onto her dinner plate.

Emma's religious beliefs were the only thing that they hadn't seen eye to eye on in the early days of their relationship, and James knew better than to ask her about it as the years went on. It became a silent wall between them. James thought that Emma knew that he would overrule her, if push came to shove. After all, it was James who had taken Finn to the hospital when he had broken his arm and needed an operation to have it pinned.

A couple of months ago, James had left the Daily Mail on the kitchen table, hoping that it would catch Emma's eye. A young Australian boy had been denied his request to refuse a life-saving blood transfusion. He was seventeen years old - just shy of his eighteenth birthday. For once, James had thought that there was a fine line. The boy didn't want the blood, and he was only weeks away from his eighteenth birthday. Giving the blood was, surely, a violation of his wishes, especially since he seemed to have such a strong faith. James knew the sanctity of life was of upmost importance to a Witness. Yet, surely to lose someone you love, like that, would be unbearable. To lose someone you love because of something that could have been prevented was too much for James and his conscience. Could you really accept someone's beliefs if acceptance meant that you would be letting them go? He had struggled to get his head around it over the years that he had been with Emma. He could not let her go like that.

"In the last few years, Emma has become...lapsed. She must not have removed the medical codicil?" James asked Mr. Abraham, waiting for confirmation.

"No. But as her next-of kin, in this case, you become her power of attorney. All decisions - medical or otherwise - must be cleared by you," Mr. Abraham replied.

"Then you carry on as you are. If she needs blood transfusions, she gets blood transfusions. I want my wife to live, to watch our children grow. I'll do *anything* I can to make that possible," James told him, assertively, once more looking directly into his eyes.

There was no point in being indecisive, was there? James didn't want Mr. Abraham to think he had any doubts, not when Emma's life was in jeopardy. Not when this was a matter of life and death. He couldn't afford to waiver on this.

"Please though, let me be the one to discuss this with her parents. They are not as... lapsed. They come from a long family history of Witnesses and they have a strong faith. They would take this news very badly if it came from a stranger," James added.

Mr. Abraham nodded in agreement. James was sure he must have dealt with this situation dozens of times over his years as a consultant, sure that he'd had to endure many difficult conversations with people who had such strong beliefs. The Witnesses were probably at the top of the list of people that he dreaded ending up on his operating table. They were risky patients. It would surely be the surgeons head on the block if something happened to them during a medical procedure? Or maybe the surgeon could use the Witnesses beliefs as an easy way out - as a way of hiding their own incompetence? People are so quick to blame these days. It's rare that someone will admit they have made a mistake when you could easily blame someone else.

James hoped he was making the right choice. He hoped that Bob and Mary, Emma's parents, would understand the choice that he had just made for Emma. But most of all, he hoped that when Emma woke up, she wouldn't hate him for this.

*

James stayed with Emma for as long as he could, before they wanted to carry on with more testing. His parents, Meg and Eric, had arrived a little while before and had set up camp in the ICU waiting room, which was for other relatives. You could only have two people by her bedside at once, and the medical staff had been in and out like yo-yos all morning, carrying out various different assessments, which made it difficult for extra visitors to sit by Emma's bed. Meg and Eric were happy to be entertaining Millie instead.

While Emma went for the tests, James and his parents wandered down to the hospital cafeteria, which was near the main entrance to the hospital. He felt that it was strange, wandering back into normality when his world was suddenly so far from normal. He picked at his sandwich while Millie devoured some pasta. James tried to fill his Mum and Dad in as much as he could on the medical side of things; he was beginning to pick things up that the doctors were saying to each other while he sat by Emma's bedside, though sometimes he wished that he hadn't heard anything at all. It didn't look good.

One of James's Dad's close friends was a retired police officer - and Eric said that he would give his friend a call, to find out if he knew anything that they didn't – to see if an investigation was underway and if they knew anything about the car that had knocked Emma and left her for dead.

During lunch, James called Emma's parents, Mary and Bob, and they said that they were going to come down to Preston right away. He gave his Mum a list of people to call. He couldn't face it all by himself. Emma would have laughed at that - at a fully-grown man relying on his mother, but what else could he do? People had to know, and he just couldn't face it.

James's parents decided as they were finishing lunch, that they were going to head back to Ambleside with Millie, collect Poppy and Finn from school, make some dinner, and put them in the bath. James told them he would try to make it back home before their bedtime if Emma was stable enough to be left for the evening.

"Try not to worry about them," his Mum, Meg, said to him kindly.

"Focus on Emma. She needs you now. The children will be just fine."

Chapter Four

When James walked back into the Intensive Care Unit, it looked like they were moving another patient into another bed in a side room. He tried not to focus as they were attaching the new patient to all the wires, while there were doctors were coming in and out. It must be hard, he thought to himself, having to witness such devastation on a day-to-day basis. How could you turn off after your shift? How could you go home and not worry about the people you have left behind? How could you not wonder if they will still be there, alive, in the morning? Or maybe, they don't wonder at all. Maybe it's better not to dwell on it, not to have expectations for a full recovery.

A nurse had brushed Emma's hair while he was away eating lunch. She had done a good job of removing most of the dried blood that had once seemed matted into her hair. It's funny, the little things you notice. James had always thought that Emma had such beautiful hair. She would be pleased that someone had taken the time to care for it, to brush out all the tangles. James made a mental note to thank the nurse, when he saw her again, maybe ask her to put it in a plait to keep it tidy while she was lying still in her hospital bed. Emma would like that.

As he sat beside his wife, James wondered how they were going to manage from here - as a family. How would he cope if Emma never recovered? Or, if she recovered in mind but became permanently physically disabled? The Parker's house was an old rambling cottage with narrow doorways and smaller-than-normal rooms. Even worse, the house itself was a good half a mile out of Ambleside. *Who could do this to her?* James wondered. *Who could knock down a woman and never look back?*

James barely had time to dwell on his thoughts before Emma's parents, Bob and Mary, walked in. Mary held James for a moment longer than she usually would, like a mother would hold a small child. Gently, but lovingly. Mary always had a calming presence, unlike James's own mother. Nothing was a rush for her and no detail could be overlooked. Things were simply the way they were. With them, they had brought Emma's ipod and a collection of old photographs from when Emma and her sister Sophie had been little girls.

"We thought you might like these? Emma can listen to the music. We can talk to her about the photographs. I'm sure that she'll feel our presence," Mary said. James hadn't even thought about that. To him, Emma was here, but not here – unconscious and unaware of the world around her.

Mary placed the earphones in Emma's ears and pressed shuffle. James waited, poised for a response.

Nothing changed.

"James, can we go and get a cup of tea?" Mary asked. He eyed her suspiciously, but knew that he could not really refuse. "I'd like to talk to you about Emma, about what she might want. Bob will stay here with her while we're gone. It won't take long." She smiled softly, unworried and unphased by what may lay ahead.

James looked at Bob, who nodded his approval. He would have to tell Mary about the conversation he'd had with Mr. Abraham about the blood transfusions and suddenly he wasn't looking forward to it. He wasn't looking forward to the argument that could follow. It is hard, isn't it, to disagree with your in-laws - especially when they were not just talking about something trivial such as where they should buy the children's shoes from, or how often they should mow the lawn. James would be talking about life and death in their own immediate family, about the life and death of the person that surely they all loved the most.

James and Mary walked together back to the canteen. James ordered a coffee and a tea and joined Mary, who had found a little table at the back of the restaurant, where they wouldn't be overheard too much by others.

Really, James felt he needed something stronger and he would have suggested it to anyone else, but Bob and Mary did not drink. Come to think of it - he wasn't entirely sure why. It certainly wasn't forbidden in the eyes of the other Witnesses, James was sure. He had seen several of their Witness friends drink at parties that they had been to at their house over the years.

Maybe they just didn't like it? Too much of something can be a bad thing, which is what his own mother had often said to him when he was a boy. James's Dad knew a retired doctor who never touched a drop of anything, except the occasional sherry on a very special occasion. He said that he owed it to his patients to have steady hands.

He looked across the table at Mary. He began to explain to her the position Emma was in when they had found her on the side of the road that morning, the multiple injuries, the trauma to her head and spine. He then told her about the conversation that he'd had with Dr. Abraham, the conversation about transfusions, about giving Emma blood if she *really* needed it.

James wondered how Mary was going to react, what she was going to say. There was nothing anyone could do now though, was there? The damage had already been done. They could be pumping Emma full of blood, right at this very moment, all because James had allowed it.

"James, I will never condemn any decision you make for our daughter. She is your wife and there is no doubt in our minds that you have her long-term interests at heart," she began.

"In trauma cases, particularly when the patient isn't carrying a medical card, it's near impossible to know that the patient *might* abstain from blood transfusions. The majority of the population, after all, have no problem with receiving blood. But it's lucky that they checked her files and realised that the codicil was in place. The medics act in the moment and in that moment sometimes they do give blood to a Witness, even though it isn't what they want. It becomes beyond their control. We make peace with it if and when it does happen, which is more often than you might think, especially when people go out and about without their medical disclaimer, which is why we always insist that our brothers and sisters carry it with them at all times."

James watched her as she sipped her tea. He hadn't expected such understanding, although, with hindsight, he wondered why. Mary had always been a welcoming and understanding person. She looked after the children one day a week, while himself and Emma were both out at work, because she wanted to out of the goodness of her heart, not because she felt duty-bound or obliged. James's own parents were great at showering the children with expensive toys and sweets every time they visited but all it really achieved was that the children expected it of them. The children became greedier and more selfish. Mary and Bob had a kinder, softer approach towards their grandchildren. The children certainly didn't love them any less because of it.

"Mary, can I ask you something?" James asked, hardly wondering if he should be asking this question to the one person who could give him the answer he didn't want to hear.

"Emma didn't carry her medical card around with her. I don't remember exactly why or when, but it's been in her bedside table for a good couple of years now. How do I know... how do I know what she would really want?"

"You'll never really know, James. Emma has always been herself, always indecisive. Little things bothered her when she was a child. Bob used to say that she was overly sensitive. I know that she hasn't been to the Kingdom Hall in some time. I asked her about it once and she shrugged it off. She was non-committal," Mary replied, taking another sip of her tea before continuing.

"You must have spoken to her about it, at some point? About abstaining from blood transfusions? Before you were married?" she asked James with a certainty to her soft voice.

He nodded in agreement.

"In the early days, when she first told me, I found it...difficult. Emma was just a normal woman. I'd always thought that Jehovah's Witnesses were a bit...strange..."

Mary chuckled. "Yes, we often hear that when we are out and about, calling on people. It's like some people expect us not to be human, like we are brainwashed - or doing things against our will. As if we aren't just normal people living completely normal lives."

"Well, as time went on we agreed to disagree. I couldn't understand it. I mean, it's not like people are just having blood transfusions for the sake of it, is it? We are talking about sick and vulnerable people. People who really need blood in order to help them to survive. Later, when Emma was pregnant with Finn it came up again in conversation. I told her that I couldn't watch my child die because someone else believed that a blood transfusion was wrong. I couldn't stand by and let a child die all the time knowing that a transfusion would save their life. Finn was just a baby; he didn't have his own ideas about things yet. If he were a grown man, and he had decided for himself not to have a transfusion, that that would be a bit different. But surely, it is a bit wrong to force your beliefs on someone who has no beliefs for themselves? When you take the choice of living away from someone who in all likelihood would choose to live. I remember that Emma nodded her head at me, but she didn't agree or disagree, and she didn't try to explain her belief any further. She didn't tell me that I was wrong, that she would fight me over making the children abstain from transfusions if it was absolutely necessary. By the time she was pregnant with Millie; her medical disclaimer was already in her bedside table..."

James let his voice trail off. What else could he say? He didn't want to rock the boat too much with his in-laws. He understood they had different beliefs, but how do you reconcile in such a situation? How do you do what is right for everyone? He looked across at Mary as she began to speak.

"We had a sister in our congregation when Finn was a baby. I am supposing that Emma never told you about her or maybe only mentioned her to you in passing. Her name was Erica Jones. She was a young woman who was married, with two little boys and, like you, her husband was not a Witness. Erica had a rare blood disease, and as time went on, she became sicker and sicker. She'd had several bloodless surgeries in Halifax to no avail. Her body simply could not regenerate new blood properly and the blood that it was managing to regenerate was of such a poor quality that it was making her very ill. Without a transfusion and subsequent regular transfusions, she would die. Her husband was not a Witness and so, eventually, he took her to court over it because, quite simply, he wanted her to live. He was torn between knowing that there was a cure out there, something that would keep her living, and letting his wife have her wishes respected. In any ideal world, you would have both but for Erica it came down to one or the other. In the end it was simply too late. His wife was gone before the judge could make that decision. Emma took her death very badly. We had the funeral at the Kingdom Hall and it was just awful. She knew Erica well; her children used to play with Poppy when she used to bring her to the Kingdom Hall every weekend. Bob and I talked about it at length afterwards and we believe that for Emma, it was just too much. Too close to home. Of course, she believed in the sanctity of life but at what cost? I think Emma knew there and then that she couldn't refuse a transfusion if it would leave her children motherless. Erica's boys had been lively, little souls when she was alive but after she was gone, they had this sad, haunting look. Emma knew that she would do what she had to do if it meant that she would be able to watch her children grow. Bob thinks that's when she started to withdraw a little from her faith, from our brothers and sisters, because she knew, in her heart of hearts, that her faith wasn't strong enough. That she simply wouldn't be able to say no. Perhaps now we will never know..." Mary let her voice trail off.

A silence hung between them for a few moments before James spoke,

"What would you do, Mary? What do I tell the doctors when I don't really know what she would want?"

"Emma is stable now, James. Bloodless surgery has come a long way in recent years and I imagine that you barely know a thing about it. They have all this equipment at their fingertips – oxygen therapy, cell-saver machines. People are opting for bloodless surgery now because it is seen as the *best* that medicine can offer. Recovery is much faster, there is a fifty percent decrease in postoperative infections, reduced mortality, shorter hospital stays, less complications, and lower costs. Can you imagine how careful a surgeon is going to be when he has a Witness on his table? How much more care he is going to take during the operation? We will support you in whatever you decide, James, but you have to really ask yourself what Emma would want. I know that some Witnesses who have been given an emergency transfusion and their position on not accepting such transfusions wasn't known until much later, well – they feel violated. They feel as if the medical profession has not taken them seriously, that their wishes have not been upheld, that their worth as a person therefore doesn't matter. All we ask is that you talk to us if things do change - if Emma's prognosis worsens and blood really is the only thing that will save her."

"I will. Thank you," he said to Mary.

They quickly finished their drinks and walked back to the ICU.

James was going to have to find Mr. Abraham immediately and see that the codicil remained in place. It might not be what he wanted, but all of this was just an emotional minefield for him. Mary was right - if the time came for Emma to need a blood transfusion they would discuss it then. They shouldn't make any rash heat of the moment decisions when emotions were running this high. He needed time to think, he needed time to wonder about what Emma would really want.

As he walked into the ICU for the third time that day, James was both relieved and yet equally horrified to find his wife exactly as he had left her.

Chapter Five

James arrived back in Ambleside at just gone seven o'clock that first evening. He felt torn between the guilt of leaving his wife in the hospital alone and coming back home to his children.

Emma was still stable, though he was beginning to realise that even 'stable' had a continuum and that there was *'she's just made it into stable'* compared to *'we are confident that she isn't going to get any worse.'*

From what James could gather, Emma was somewhere in the middle. Mr. Abraham said he was confident she would have a quiet night – she was heavily medicated and still totally out of touch with what was going on in the real world. *Go home, get some rest, you're going to need it,* he had told James. Although James knew that sleep wouldn't come easily to him that night, he knew that Mr. Abraham was right. If nothing else, James felt that he really ought to explain something to his children.

James's parents had everything in order as he walked through the door. The smell of baby shampoo filled the living room; the hens had long since been locked in for the night. His Dad was reading a story to Poppy and Finn while Millie was playing with her toys on the floor. His Mum put a plate of pie in front of him, telling him that he needed to keep up his strength. James picked at it, filling her in on the afternoon at the hospital – the results of the brain scan and the conversation with Mary.

James and his mother talked about the practicalities of the next few days. Meg insisted on staying in the spare room - so that if he needed to be at the hospital late, or was called in the middle of the night he could just leave without a second thought. His mother would coordinate the school runs and afterschool clubs, cook the meals, and wash the uniforms. James's parents lived in Windermere, which was the next village along, but they had long since retired. He supposed that, in another few days another schedule would have to be drawn up for Mary and Bob. The children would have to be divided between the two sets of grandparents if this was really going to work as a long-term solution. James would have to call Hannah too, and enlist her help, as the children loved her happy-go-lucky approach to life, and she was often at a loose end in the evenings anyway.

First, James called work and told them that he would be taking a leave of absence, that he didn't know how long it would last - or when he would be coming back to work because he didn't really have a prognosis for Emma yet. It could be days or weeks before that happened but that could easily slip into months, maybe even years. *'Don't worry about your workload. You're covered for six months of full pay. Take as much time as you need'* his boss had told him. It was yet another thing that James had managed to overlook – how they would manage to weather this storm financially. Although Emma didn't need to work, per se, her salary certainly made a big difference to the Parker household. He made another mental note to call Emma's boss first thing in the morning.

Sitting down with the children was harder than he would ever have dared to imagine. Of course, they loved their mother. There weren't any answers as to *why* the car had knocked her down and how long it was going to take for Emma to get better. James told them that their mother was very sick, that he didn't know how long it would take her to get better, or if she would ever get better again. He told them that the doctors would do everything they could to help her, but that sometimes trying your best just isn't enough. He told them that, at the moment, she was too sick for them to visit, but they could draw pictures and send presents for her to have by her bed, where she was resting.

Poppy nodded, acceptingly. James was sure that his Mum and Dad had spoken to her after school. Poppy had always been an inquisitive child - she needed to know plans and reasons for things; she liked to know what was going on and when. Finn ran upstairs and found his lion, the lion he'd had since he was a tiny boy, the tatty old lion that went everywhere with him. It was only recently that Emma had managed to persuade him that the lion didn't need to go to school with him every day, that lion could be left at home and he wouldn't be upset or mind – he would like being in charge of all the other toys.

"Lion will look after Mummy," he said, handing the tattered lion to his father. James tried his hardest not to burst into tears and collapse in front of his son. He held Finn tightly, for a moment longer than he would usually allow, before Finn ran off to find his supper.

James collapsed on the sofa and he started to make more calls. It all still felt surreal. Less than twenty-four hours ago, their lives had been perfect. The Parkers were just an average family living an average lifestyle.

People responded to James's call with a mixture of shock and confusion. He lost count of all the *I'm so sorry* and *if there's anything I can do*.... He didn't want peoples' sympathy. He wanted his wife to be fit and well. He wanted to turn back the clock so that this had never happened.

One thought had remained strong in James's mind during all this time. He wanted answers. He wanted justice to be sought, for the guilty ones to be punished for this hideous crime against his family. He knew he wouldn't sleep again at night knowing that the person who had done this was still out there, somewhere. Perhaps even biding his time to do it again.

There was only one thing that James felt he could do now. He picked up his car keys and set off towards the police station.

*

Ambleside police station had long since officially closed. Not enough crime, James had assumed. Years ago, when Emma was a child, the station had a manned desk, but eventually that had dwindled and they moved all of the police officers to Windermere because that station was much larger - though even that was only manned now in the mornings.

The whole area was now policed by what was known as Central Lakes, and if anything major occurred then you had to go to Kendal, which was fifteen miles away, to be met by someone at a desk. They had holding cells in Kendal, but it still wasn't a big station by any standards.

The A591 was the road that ran right through the Lake District, yet it was quiet as James drove through to Kendal that evening, and the weather was already beginning to turn cold for the night. There would be a hard frost tomorrow, but there hadn't been one in a couple of days. The weather had been oddly warm for December, warmer than usual but still very wet. He shuddered to think about Emma, lying unconscious and alone on that road – it was bad enough as it was, but the winters here were bitter. Emma was lucky not to have ended up with hypothermia, luckier still that the forecast for heavy snow had never materialised.

James parked the car at the front of the car park, and walked straight in through the main door. He wondered if the people in Kendal had even heard about the accident yet, as he began telling the events to the woman sat at the desk who looked like she was young enough to still be in full-time education. She informed James that an officer would come and talk to him when they were 'free' – so he took a seat and waited.

Nearly twenty minutes later, two officers showed him to a side room. James supposed that they had to work in twos to cover their backs, to make sure that the person they were talking to didn't suddenly come up with an elaborate story of events.

The last time he had been in a police station was years ago, when a drunk driver crashed into his car and he had to produce the obligatory documents after the accident. This was a completely different league for James, something that didn't even come close.

"P.C. Smith and this is P.C. Scott," the older of the two officers said to him, offering his hand and gesturing towards the seat.

James answered a few simple questions first, filling in forms and ticking all those boxes. Emma's date of birth, height, weight, hair colour, the possessions she had on her, and the clothes she was wearing when he had last seen her.

They wanted to know where James was that evening and what he had been doing, and James paused for a moment. He had read far too many crime novels in his time to know that they wanted to eliminate him as a suspect. James told them he had been at home looking after the children, marking papers and that his mother had popped in briefly to collect her purse, which she had left behind that afternoon.

He immediately felt guilty. James had nothing to hide, so why did he lie? They would find no evidence against him, nothing to put him at the scene of the crime, because, quite simply, he had not been there. More importantly, Emma was his wife. He wouldn't have even wished this on his worst enemy.

P.C. Smith then told James that they had put up a *sign*. He actually thought they were joking for a moment, but no. No one had come forward with any information, so they had put up a sign appealing for witnesses. He almost laughed at the stupidity of it. Whoever had knocked Emma down hadn't given her more than a backwards glance. They had wanted to hurt her, cause her pain. They certainly didn't want her to survive. James thought that it was extremely unlikely that someone was going to walk into the police station and confess to their crime.

The officers asked James if he knew of anyone who had a grudge against Emma, and his mind hit a blank wall. He couldn't think of anyone. Had she upset a patient at work? Had she ever had a major fall-out with an old boyfriend or a friend from school? James shook his head. He told them that Emma had been adopted, but that wasn't a big secret and was more common than you would think, wasn't it, these days? Mary and Bob had told Emma the truth from a very young age. No, he told them, she does not have any contact with her biological parents, because she never wanted to. Mary and Bob are the only parents she knows and loves, and the only parents that Emma wanted to know. He told them that they hadn't even told the children about it and that it certainly never came up in day-to-day conversation. James saw the younger officer making a note on a piece of paper.

"It's best to check all avenues of enquiry, Mr. Parker," the other added, as they began to move on to people Emma knew in her everyday life – her friends, her family, her colleagues. They informed

James that they would make contact with them all, to make sure that nothing was untoward, but, at the moment, they weren't treating the accident as suspicious.

"More likely a drink driving accident, we suspect," he said.

"It happens a lot more than you would like to think - especially around here. People go out to the pub for a couple of pints and think its okay to drive home. They don't think that the fact that they can't walk straight is a good indication that they shouldn't get in the car and start the engine. Instead, they are thinking about the inconvenience of having to walk back into town and collect the car in the morning. They think that, in this day and age, in a rural area with little crime, it would be very *unlucky* if they were pulled over by the police."

James could hardly believe it, the fact that they thought they were right in their assumptions, or the fact that they didn't seem interested in investigating the real cause of the accident.

The smaller officer, P.C. Scott, sensing his discomfort, added,

"We've got extensive pictures of the crime scene. Someone with more experience is going to have a look at the road tomorrow. We are still waiting for a report from the hospital about the extent of your wife's injuries. We will look into it all, Mr. Parker; we assure you. If anything suspicious is evident, we will begin to start looking into things with a lot more detail."

James left the station that night with more questions than answers.

He left thinking that this is not at all how they would have gone about this on *Scott and Bailey*. This isn't the gritty determination that he would have expected from a department that seems to have no problem in taking so much of his money in taxes every year. It was time to call in any favours he had. He would do this properly. He owed it to Emma, to the children.

James would find out who had hurt his wife - and why.

Chapter Six

The next two days passed James by in a haze.

Emma was still alive, and he had to remind himself each evening (as he prepared for another night of restless sleep), that was all that mattered. That Emma hadn't given up; that she was fighting with every little bit of strength she had left.

Emma's PET scan wasn't showing the results that the doctors had hoped. In fact, there were indications of acute traumatic brain injury, and there was no way of knowing how her recovery would go from here.

James clung to any glimmer of hope that he was offered – that the younger you are at the time of injury the better your chances for a full recovery, that fifty percent of all patients go on to live life *almost exactly* as they had before. Emma was still being kept alive by the ventilator, by the tubes that pumped liquid into her veins. She was still unresponsive.

He spent his days sitting by Emma's bedside, willing her to get better, and writing any thoughts he had down in his notebook. He spent his evenings trying to keep life as normal as he could for their children. Trying to be there, reading the schoolbooks, helping them with their homework, washing their hair, and kissing them goodnight.

Once the children were asleep, James then spent his evenings making call after call to no avail. Nobody could recollect anything strange about

Emma in those weeks leading up to the accident. Even Hannah had seemed shocked when he had suggested to her that Emma had told him that she didn't feel safe, that she thought she was being watched. *She would have told me James, if she thought it was something serious*, Hannah had told him. It became yet another thing that he simply had to believe.

Mary and Bob had come to Ambleside to take over from James's mother, Meg, for a few days. It was Thursday now, the fourth day since the accident, and the weekend was looming. The police had made no great leaps and bounds with their sign that appealed for witnesses. No drunk drivers had been in and confessed to their crime. It added further salt to the wound. If anything, it made James even more determined than ever to find out the truth.

James thought that the children were coping remarkably well, all things considering. Every morning, they handed over pictures for him to take to their mother. He didn't have the heart to tell them that the pictures first had to be laminated and sprayed in alcohol before they were even considered sterile enough to be placed in the ICU by their mother's bedside. It made him mad that a painted egg box had to be left behind carelessly at the ICU reception desk, a gift for her mother that Poppy had spent ages decorating with glitter and beads. It made James mad because Emma was sick, really sick. Surely, one little painted egg box wouldn't make any difference to that?

The local Primary School that the children attended, Ambleside Primary, had organised for a children's councillor to come to the Parker's house after school and talk to the children about their ailing mother. James was sceptical about the amount of good it would do, but the school insisted that they wanted a report to show that the children were minimally affected by this disruption to their lives. That they had procedures in place if the children were not coping as well as it seemed. That they had ticked all of their boxes.

The woman who was conducting the report was thorough but friendly, and although James saw her as an intrusion, a hindrance rather than a help, he would be grateful for her presence in the days that were yet to come. Grateful for the kind words she would write about his family.

It's just what you do though, isn't it? He thought. Families look after each other in times of trouble; they rally together and protect those who are most vulnerable. It was funny that he never included himself in this vulnerability. James thought that because he was an adult, and he was, therefore, able to rationalise his own thoughts and feelings that such support was unnecessary for him. But maybe the school were right - the children needed protection and support. The children needed to know that they were loved and that just because their mother wasn't there with them right now, didn't mean that she should be forgotten.

On that Thursday afternoon, James left the hospital earlier than usual. Emma's condition had remained largely the same. Her sister, Sophie, who lived on the other side of Kendal to Mary and Bob, was happy to go through to Preston and sit with her until the evening. James told Mary and Bob not to worry about the children tonight, that he would collect them all from their various establishments and look after them by himself. He thought that it would signify a little touch of normal in their otherwise chaotic lives.

Trying to ignore the other parents pitiful looks at the school gates, James managed to pick up Poppy and Finn without too much drama. Together, after collecting Millie from nursery, they walked slowly back to the house through the park. It was cold, and the Parker family were all togged up in their winter wear. James decided that he would call for a pizza delivery that night and let the children have a bit of a treat. Pizza delivery was a new thing to the village and had only been open a few months, but the Parkers had already managed to establish themselves as regular customers. It was yet another thing people in cities take for granted – the multitude of takeaways that they can have delivered free to their door.

James, Poppy, Finn, and Millie were all munching on their overload of cheese when the doorbell rang. James almost ignored it, but living just outside of the village meant that someone wouldn't really stop by on the chance that they were in, not unless the callers knew them, unless they were family or friends. The Parker house was simply too far out for people who were just passing. Reluctantly, he got up and went to open the door.

James had never met the woman who was standing in front of him before and at first, he didn't really understand who she was and why he couldn't place her.

"James Parker?" she asked, cautiously.

"Yes?" he replied.

"Rachel Jackson...I've come to talk about Poppy...," she said with a wobbly voice, with even more hesitation than the first time.

He studied her, looked her straight in the eye. James should have slammed the door shut in her face, told her and her husband to get a good lawyer. He should have gone back to dinner with his family and given her no more than a passing thought, which is all that James thought she deserved.

But for some odd reason, he didn't.

For some very strange reason, he invited the stranger into his house, into his life. For some very strange reason he thought that he could talk some sense into a woman that he didn't know, that perhaps she must have some kind of compassion to come all this way to talk about the well-being of Poppy, when it would have been much easier to pick up the phone.

James wished that he could tell you that his instincts were right, but they weren't. Rachel Jackson's words would haunt him for days to come. Her words would bring about the second most devastating thing that could happen to his family in less than a week.

Yet, unbeknown to all of this, he offered her a chair, a cup of tea – even a slice of pizza, would you believe?

James owed her nothing, and yet he extended his hospitality to her. That's what a good person would do, isn't it? Think objectively and weigh up all the facts without prejudice. James decided that he would form his own ideas about this woman, instead of listening to those around him. Instead of listening to the people he loved.

He sat down and listened to her story.

Time stood still.

For the second time in a matter of days, James Parker's world collapsed.

FIVE DAYS LATER

Chapter Seven

James found the purple folder tucked in the cupboard. It was the cupboard in which Emma kept all the important documents.

It was nine days after the still unknown car had knocked her down. Nine days of living in a nightmare. Nine days of waking up each morning, wishing, hoping that this was all a bad dream – that Emma would be lying sleepily beside him every morning, as she usually was.

For a few days now, James had been putting off going into this cupboard - going to find the documents that the lawyer wanted to see – Poppy's change of name deeds, her birth certificate, her passport. He was putting it off, because he didn't want to answer the questions that were coming. He didn't want to accept that the people who had shunned her for most of her life so far, could suddenly want her back. That the nightmare he currently found himself in could suddenly get a whole lot worse.

James and Emma had talked about adoption once or twice over the years, and either the time was too soon or they couldn't be bothered with the endless amount of paperwork that it would entail. Mostly, James wanted revenge on the man who seemed to be able to care so little for his own flesh and blood. Making him contribute to Poppy financially meant that at least once a month he had to think about her - maybe he had to go without something that he really wanted, because the law in the United Kingdom clearly stated that a proportion of Poppy's father's earnings should be paid towards her upbringing. Child maintenance, they called it. It was only right, both Emma and James agreed, that Poppy didn't miss out on things just because her biological father wasn't around.

It went without saying that James had never seen the folder before. He didn't like to mess with Emma's organisation system because she was meticulous at keeping things in order. Everything was filed away, oldest at the back and newest at the front just in case she wanted to check their electricity bill from five years ago, or wanted to look at an old school report belonging to the children.

The important things in the cupboard - passports, birth certificates, and their marriage certificate lived in another folder, which was red, which was the one that James was really looking for. The red folder also housed Emma's life insurance policy and will, which James knew she had meant to change since they married but had never actually got round to doing. James needed to read it over, make sure that he did things as best as he could given the circumstances. He wanted to make sure that things were as his wife wanted them to be.

You see, as if things weren't bad enough for James, Emma was beginning to slip away from him. She had stabilised after those first couple of days in the hospital, but since then her statistics had been dropping. Her prognosis wasn't good - severe brain damage, paralysis down her left side. Her internal organs were beginning to fail one by one. There was nothing they could do for her now except make her comfortable. It wasn't a case of 'if' anymore. It was a more definite case of 'when.'

James wondered, to himself, how long this purple folder had been in the cupboard, and why he hadn't noticed it before, as he pulled it out. To anyone else, there was nothing odd about the folder – it was just another folder in a cupboard full of them. There was nothing about its plainness that made it stand out any more than any of the others. But Emma liked systems – blue was for bills, green was for medical.

Purple did not figure in her arrangements.

Purple had no place in this cupboard.

When James first opened the folder, he was surprised by its lack of order. Papers seemed to have been thrown in carelessly. There appeared to be a large amount of papers written by Emma with her usual, neat handwriting. Some kind of reports were tucked in the middle. Emma had written a cover note, haphazardly, with a pencil. James shouldn't have been surprised by this, except that she usually hated writing with pencils. Her writing colour of choice was a blue biro. James was always sent out to buy new black biros for the children's passports, and it always annoyed her that she had to conform to something she didn't like.

There were still things about the accident that, for James, didn't make sense. His wife was a loving, caring woman. Who would knock her down in the middle of the night and leave her for dead? The police were still writing it off as a drunk-driver incident, but there hadn't been much proof or evidence to support their claims. There was no driver that could be held accountable. No one had come forward with any information.

The Parkers lived in a small village, and James found the lack of forthcoming information especially hard to swallow. People looked out for each other here; people's lives had real value. People saw James around in the days after the accident; saw him dropping Poppy and Finn off at school in the mornings, struggling with Millie as he tried to drop her off at day-care with a minimal amount of fuss. Surely, if the local people knew something about what had happened to Emma, they would speak out, wouldn't they?

It just didn't make any sense.

Yet, the more that James thought about it, the more he started to believe that Emma was right. That she knew that someone had been following her, watching her. He remembered telling his wife that she had been reading too many *Stephen King* books, that she had such a wild, over reactive imagination. He had shoved her playfully, Emma had given him that look, and then she didn't mention it to him again.

Now, she was lying there in the hospital, miles away from where she belonged. She was helpless, dying. Right now, if there was an award for the most rubbish husband, James thought that he would certainly win hands down.

Maybe, he thought, as he ran his finger over the edges of the purple folder, maybe this was where the answers began?

It was late at night now but James knew that, yet again, sleep wouldn't come easily to him. It was surprising, he thought, how the body could cope with lack of sleep when it's pushed to the limit. Surprising how much your body can adjust.

James silently wondered to himself, in those long drives twice a day to Preston hospital and back to Ambleside, if the Parker family would ever adjust after this? Could he ever accept that what had happened really was an accident, or would he be plagued by these ill feelings for the rest of his days?

He braced himself.

He took a deep breath.

He opened the folder, and he began to read...

Chapter Eight

Dear James,

If you are reading this letter, then something bad has happened to me and I was right. Please don't wallow on it - what's done is done. This isn't your fault. It's about what happens next that matters – it's about finding the answers, and protecting our family.

How can I begin to explain my worries to you? As I'm writing this there seem so many. Mum and Dad will help you with the children – please let them do their bit. They will want to help.

You can survive without me, though I imagine that you would rather not think about it – having to survive without me that is. If it's any consolation, I would rather this wasn't happening either but you know as well as I do, that you can't run from your fears – that you have to face them, head on.

You and I have come so far from the places that I've been as a child. Haunting memories that plagued my nightmares and still don't make sense to me as an adult. Recently, I've been wondering if they have anything to do with why I am being followed. That maybe decoding my memories might help you in some way. I'm sorry that it's up to you to decode them. I am not sure if the authorities will be able to help, but there are reports in the back of this folder for you to read. Reports from the psychologist that I had to see when I was a little girl, when the nightmares were at their worst.

Mum will help you as much as she can, but I fear that she doesn't have the real answers either. They just had to put up with all my sleepless nights - in the hope that they would go away with time, back then, isn't what it is today – all open and honest. Prospective parents weren't told much, if anything, about the children they came to love as their own. My childhood is a mystery that we have never solved. I am sure that it holds some kind of key to all of this, that something will make things suddenly click into place.

There's something else that you and I have never discussed. Something that, until recently, had become another painful memory for me, a time that my brain liked to forget. Disassociation, it's called. It's when your body detaches itself from a memory or an experience that is too painful to process. It's when your body shuts the experience out, closes a door in your brain, and locks it firmly with a key. Entering the door could bring your whole world crashing down, if you try to enter it again.

I'm talking about the baby that I lost all those years ago. I haven't been able to speak about her to you because, well, what would be the point? There's no point in dragging up the past. What's gone is gone.

Besides, it's hardly something you can bring up over dinner is it – that a long long time ago I had a baby and she died. I don't want pity, but that's what I would get. I didn't want to talk about how much it upset me, about all the medication I took to numb the pain. It goes without saying that it was the most difficult time of my life.

Only last year, something very strange and unexpected happened. A letter came through our door. The letter was from one of the other parents who had a sick baby in the hospital at the same time as me. She wrote to tell me that she thought they could have done more for Iris. That the hospital could have done more to help her survive, that is.

Iris was taken from me when she was such a tiny baby, James, when she was only a few days old. I think that Joe was relieved when we heard the news about her illness. We didn't know if she would survive the birth. We didn't know if we would get to hold her, love her, if she would ever take her first breath. It was a very dark, sad time for me.

After Iris was gone, Joe thought that it was better for me to 'get over it' and 'move on with my life'.

But I couldn't.

I wanted to remember her. I didn't want her to be forgotten or lost. I didn't want her life to be meaningless. Sometimes, when I remember how Joe was back then, I'm glad that Poppy has grown up without him, although I know that's a terrible thing for me to say about the man who gave her life. Joe can be cruel and thoughtless. He didn't care about other people, not me, and certainly not Iris – he only cared about himself.

I should have told you then, James. I know that now. I was wrong to keep something like this from you for all of this time. But we had just had

Millie, you were busy at work – working late and working weekends. We had three small children under five – how could I explain to you my desperate need to find out the truth about Iris's life, which may have been cut too short? How would that make any difference to us now?

So I went to see the woman who had sent me the letter – Jean Witton. She lives just outside Morecambe. It's not far from us really, is it? I wonder if we have ever passed her in the park over these years with her little boy? He's nine years old now, with his whole life ahead of him. His problems weren't as serious as Iris's. He was just a tiny baby when I saw him last, frail, and weak. He was beautiful, James, so full of life. Iris has been gone for a long time now, physically, although, of course, I have often thought about her as the years went by. It was hard to see Jean's boy here now, living. Living the life that Iris never got to have.

I know what you're thinking, James. You're wondering what, if anything, Iris has to do with me being followed. To the strange things that have been happening here in the last few weeks.

I thought that too, for a while. Perhaps I am just paranoid, like you think. Perhaps you'll never need to read this letter, and perhaps all of this will just blow over.

But something deep inside me tells me that it won't.

A week after I met Jean Witton, she was found dead one night. She was hit by a passing car. Drunk driver, the police had said. There were no witnesses. Her husband was distraught. Her son was left without a mother.

It got me thinking, and not in a good way. I have to ask you, James – do you still think that all of this is a coincidence now?

If you're reading this then it can only mean that things have gone from bad to worse. I'm sorry that you have to deal with this on your own and I'm sorry that I'm not here to help. I know that you'll do the right thing.

Be strong, look after our family.

I'll miss you

Emma x x

P.S. The files in the back of this folder might come in useful. The man in charge of our adoption was called Steven Brann. I believe he still works in Chester, which is where we were legally adopted before we moved north to our new home in the Lake District with Mary and Bob.

P.P.S. The pages that follow are documents of past events that my councillor encouraged me to write to Iris. The entries dwindle over the years and the letters run as one long continuous document over time, but I thought that they might help you to understand.

Chapter Nine

I am twenty-three years old when they tell me that you're growing inside me, Iris. I've finished my nurses training, and I'm working in the Royal Manchester Children's Hospital. It's a demanding job, and I have to be on my feet all the time, working shifts, dealing with things that can be uncomfortable – children who are terminally ill. I've worked here for a few years now and I've already decided that I'd like to do a midwifery short program, which will make me a qualified midwife. The hours and pay would be better, and the job would be more flexible, more enlightening - bringing babies into the world instead of helping them to leave it in the best way possible. Plus, I would be able to move back north and live closer to my family.

Your father, Joe, isn't pleased about your arrival. I'm not sure I should be telling you this, but I am supposed to be truthful after all. We've been together for some time now, but we are young. Perhaps you might think that we have one of those relationships that doesn't really go anywhere. You're probably right. Joe is happy living in the carefree-now.

He wants me to have an abortion. I've thought about it; in fact, I've given it more than a passing thought. But I can't do it. My parents brought me up as a Jehovah's Witness. Abortion is a big no for us; it would go against everything that I believe. It would go against the sanctity of life –

because life is a precious gift to behold and not something that you can throw away, carelessly, with all the other medical waste.

So instead, as you're growing inside me, I worry about all the things that aren't perfect. Our flat is too small, in a tower block of what are supposed to be 'modern and spacious' living quarters. The reality is that they are cramped and the walls are too thin. We can hear the couple next door arguing through our living room wall, when we are trying to watch TV. The lift is permanently broken.

We should move, but I don't think that either of us can face it - it's too much hassle and would take up time and energy that neither of us have. Your father's work is erratic. He works in accounts and the pay is good but the hours are long and he has to travel across the city to reach his office. Sometimes we can go days without seeing each other when I am working nights in the hospital, crossing paths in the hallway when I am going to work and he is returning and nothing more.

The midwife does her usual checks on me when I go for my initial appointment and then I'm sent for an appointment for my twelve-week scan. You're there on the screen in front of me – a little jelly bean, a little heartbeat. Your father was too busy at work to come with me. I think he thinks that if he tries hard enough to ignore what's happening it might go away. The sonographer tells me that I'll have a more detailed scan at twenty weeks.

I carry on, working as usual. I've had to tell my boss the news and she didn't seem to mind. She told me to let her know when I want to take my maternity leave and to let her know how much time I think I'm going to have with the baby afterwards.

My parents have sent you some baby clothes in the post - soft little cream cardigans and blankets. I put them away in a cupboard. Leaving them lying around might aggravate your father and I didn't want to worsen a situation which was already becoming more and more sour.

At twenty weeks, somehow, I manage to bully your father into coming with me for the scan. I was beginning to show a little now; I'd had to go out shopping and buy jeans with an elastic waist to cope with the ever-expanding bulge that was you. I thought that if he saw you on the screen, it might make you seem more real to him. That if he could begin to accept that you were real, we could move forward from that. Looking back, if I'd have known what would follow, I certainly wouldn't have pushed him into it. Not then.

As they moved the probe across my lower abdomen, I could sense that something was wrong. Nurse's intuition maybe? Who really knows?

You were smaller than you should have been. There was something wrong – your brain hadn't developed as expected, you have a structural heart defect, and your kidneys are malformed. You have something that made you one of 6,000 births.

Edwards Syndrome.

You became female to us then, but you were so fragile. Never had a life seemed so precious.

Your condition was life threatening. As a nurse, I'd worked with children that were so sick they didn't know if they were coming or going, at the end. It was highly likely that you'd be gone before you could begin to feel anything, to have any wants or dreams.

We became surrounded by statistics that were damning and gave us very little hope for your future, Iris. The consultant told us that last year there were 496 cases of children diagnosed with Edwards Syndrome, 339 abortions, 49 stillborns, 72 unknown outcomes, 35 live births. Only eight percent of those who do survive birth live beyond their first birthday. Only one percent of children lived to be ten years old.

The consultant spoke to me slowly and factually. I could have a late -termination if I wanted. 'Medically induced abortion' was what they called it. I would still have to give birth to you but most certainly, you would be born dead. But, for me, if there was just a tiny chance of holding you alive, I couldn't do it. If there was even a one percent chance that you might defy all the odds and live to be ten years old then I had to take that chance. I couldn't fail you, Iris. I'd grown you and loved you up until now. No medical information could change that. No damning statistics.

I took the next week off from work and went to stay with my parents in Kendal, Cumbria. I felt vulnerable and weak and I needed help and support from people I trusted, from people who I knew would tell me that I was doing the right thing.

Your father seemed mainly concerned about how having you was going to limit his life and I couldn't be surrounded by such negative thoughts. I couldn't let them drag me down. We had come so far, you and I. We could get through it, couldn't we? We could weather the storms together, if we tried hard enough?

The next few months were trying. I carried on at work for as long as I could. Your father and I lived separate lives as much as it were possible for people to do so when they were both living in the same building. I volunteered for night shifts, because I knew that I would be less likely to run into him that way, and I needed the extra money. I had no idea how my life would be afterwards. I felt bad enough carrying you inside me, knowing all the time that you would most probably live for only a matter of hours, if at all.

The worst thing of all was that I had to smile and nod at strangers who asked me how long I had to go, or if you were a boy or girl. I often wondered how they would react if I had told them the bitter truth and it was at the tip of my tongue a few times. But it would have been cruel and life was cruel enough.

The hospital gave me lots of leaflets to read and DVDs to watch. I tried to take it all in. We wouldn't know how you would look, or how the birth would go. I didn't dare to have hopes about your birth, didn't dare to buy any clothes or nappies. In the last few weeks, I stayed in the flat by myself, every day, curtains drawn.

I shut out the world, just like the world had shut out you, Iris.

The day that I knew you were coming, I called your father and he came home from work. I sat by the front of the apartment block, waiting for him. He opened the car door for me. We didn't talk about what was happening, or about how we would cope afterwards. Instead, we clipped our seatbelts in a calm and orderly fashion. We drove to the hospital.

Chapter Ten

You came to me, on that Tuesday morning, like a breath of fresh air after a ten-hour delivery. You were born normally, with a little bit of gas and air.

Most importantly, Iris, you were born alive. You took your first breath without any help from a ventilator. You cried the softest and the sweetest of cries. The hospital nurses didn't waste too much time washing you and weighing you. What was the point? We didn't have the luxury of time to waste.

I held you tightly; I stroked your small hands. You looked so normal, so healthy. People wouldn't have known that there was anything wrong with you. The doctors had put us in a side room on the ward, away from the other babies, and although I could understand why, I didn't like it. I wanted you to be the same as the other babies. I didn't want you hidden, shut away, but then, I also wanted to savour every moment I had with you. I didn't want to have to explain your illness, your prognosis. I didn't want people to look at me with sad eyes and a heavy heart. I was just happy that I'd managed to see you, alive.

An hour after you had arrived with us, an hour of me holding you closely, a doctor came to talk with us. Your father had gone outside to make some calls; there didn't seem much point to that really in my mind, but I think he wanted space. He had convinced himself that you wouldn't survive the birth, so the real alive baby had come as a bit of a shock to him.

The doctor told us that we were losing you, Iris. That your heart was too defective, that you would soon have multiple organ failures. I'd have a healthy baby one day, the doctors told me as if it were some kind on consolation for what I was losing. I looked back at them, wide eyed, saying nothing.

My mother's instinct was to hold you Iris, until your last breath. To comfort you. To be there. The doctors told us that you wouldn't feel too much pain. That eventually, you would just slip away from us. We didn't argue. We didn't tell them to wire you up to the latest medical equipment that they had. What would be the point? We wanted you to be alive, not merely living.

When I said goodbye to you that morning, I didn't know that I'd have an empty hole inside of me for many years to come. Your father went and collected the car from the hospital car park.

I simply couldn't stay in the hospital on the maternity ward any longer – it would have been too much like rubbing salt in a wound, watching other women who were happy with their healthy babies. I would recover from giving birth at home, alone, without my baby. I had decided that I would take two weeks off from work; I would have two weeks of wallowing in self-pity and grief, and then I would step back out into the normal world.

If only it was that easy.

Chapter Eleven

How can I begin to explain how those early days were without you, Iris?
I am your mother. I spent nine months growing you inside me. Nine months of loving you. I came home with an empty stomach and an aching heart. My body was screaming for you, my missing baby. My breasts were full of milk, my senses heightened. I was tired and sore from the delivery. It had been less than twelve hours since I had you. Now I was back at home, eating dinner in front of Eastenders as if life hadn't changed at all. As if you'd never happened. As if you didn't matter.
Your father went back to work the day after you were born. It was as if he wanted to forget everything that had happened. He left me to deal with all of the arrangements for your funeral. I went to the funeral directors in a haze of grief. I picked out a small, white coffin. I ordered the flowers, purple and white irises to cover the top of your coffin.
When we buried you, it was rainy and damp, as if the world were crying its own tears for you. We went with a few people to a local cafe afterwards, but it all felt so wrong. How can you celebrate a life that hadn't really begun?
I plodded around the flat in my dirty pyjamas. I didn't shower, I didn't clean. Joe had sent for a doctor who had prescribed me a high dose of Prozac. It allowed me to sleep better, to

function on a more normal level. But it didn't make me happy. It just made me numb.

Joe worked late; he worked weekends, he went out with new friends from work that didn't know us. He never brought them back to the flat. I doubt he ever explained to them that he'd lost a daughter recently. Why would he? It would only prompt difficult questions that he didn't want to answer. Sometimes - I wondered if he had even told them that I'd been pregnant in the first place.

My parents encouraged me to see a counsellor. His name was Mark, and the first time I walked into his office, I thought that I was wasting his time. How could a man ever understand the pain a woman goes through when she loses her first baby? But it turned out that Mark had lost people he loved too.

I am twenty-four years old now. The days are all the same. Six months, Mark tells me, and I have to go back to work. I just stared at him the first time he had said it. Later, when I thought about it, he was right. I needed normality. I knew that I wouldn't be able to forget you, not like your father had. That I would live the rest of my life wondering how you could have been.

Gradually, I weaned myself off the medication. I started cleaning the flat, paying attention to how I looked and what I wore. I told my boss that I needed to return to work, and she didn't flinch. She didn't tell me that she didn't think I should be working with children anymore, that I might find it too upsetting. She let me get on with my job, so that's exactly what I did.

For the next two years, I remembered you, Iris. I took flowers to your grave every Friday, a wreath at Christmas. Normally, I wouldn't have celebrated these things at all but it felt right; it felt like the right thing to do. I felt like a good parent, tending to your grave. I wouldn't let people think that we didn't love you. I wouldn't let them see the inscription on your grave and think that now you were gone you were forgotten to me. You'd never be forgotten.

Looking back, I worked more hours than I should have. I volunteered myself for extra shifts, extra nights, and I put away the extra money in my own bank account. Your father didn't complain. He didn't really say much to me at all these days. Often, I wondered why we were still together. I'd wondered if I should ask him to leave, but I couldn't bring myself to do it. He was the only link I had with you, Iris. He was, I thought, the only one who could really understand.

You had been gone for nearly three years when it happened again. Pregnancy. The fact that I had fallen pregnant was surely a miracle in itself. For most of the time, your father and I slept in separate rooms. Sex became something he demanded when he was drunk, not the something that it should have been.

I took the pregnancy test by myself and made an appointment with my doctor. I needed to know what the chances were of having another baby like you, before I brought the subject up with your father.

We were in a bad place and I knew that. Our relationship couldn't cope with a baby. Perhaps your father felt obligated to stay with me after you'd gone because what was the alternative? Telling a woman, after just losing her baby, that you didn't love her anymore? That you didn't want her around? Your father was many things, but he wasn't completely heartless. Not then.

The doctor told me that the likelihood of having another baby like you was less than one percent. The odds were in my favour, this time. She prescribed me a higher than usual dose of folic acid and told me to take it twice a day. She made me an appointment with the midwife. I went to see my boss and asked for a transfer back to a hospital up north. I decided that I would go and live with my parents for a while, stay up there where I had friends and people who could help me. People that I could rely on. I still visited your grave every day, Iris. I still felt guilty that you had gone, that you might feel like I was simply replacing you with something new. It wasn't like that, Iris. You would always be my first baby.

Eventually, I told your father, but by then it was too late for him to change my mind. He couldn't wear me down with talks of abortion. He couldn't frighten me into thinking that all of this was a wasted effort, that my new baby would surely just die too.

I was stronger than I had been in a long time. I felt like I had been given another chance, a chance to be the best mother I could possibly be. I told him that I had to do what I thought was right for our baby. I told him that I would do it alone, without his help, if that were what it took. I wouldn't let my baby down. I couldn't.

The next afternoon, I packed my worldly possessions into one small suitcase and a carrier bag, and your father didn't try to stop me, or say that he was sorry. I booked a one-way ticket back home online and texted my Mum to make sure she would pick me up from the other side at Oxenholme station.

I was ready for a new life. I was ready for the challenges that would come my way. If my new baby were sick too, then I'd just deal with that, if and when it happened. I couldn't worry about the future or all the things that might not be right with my situation. I couldn't look back at this time when I was older and wish that I had made a different choice.

Without a backwards glance, I opened the door and left.

Chapter Twelve

I am twenty-six years old when I step off the train to be greeted by my mother. She knows that I'm coming back home to stay on a permanent basis, which must seem as strange for her as it does for me. My sister, Sophie, and I had been brought up in Ambleside, which is some fifteen miles north of Kendal –where my parents lived now. They had a slightly smaller house now, and they had moved in a time when property in Kendal was much cheaper than it was in the Lake District.

The main reason for the move was that they wanted to be closer to the Kingdom Hall - to their brothers and sisters in the congregation. They loved Ambleside, but the lure of amenities was too tempting for them in their old age. Dad was nearly sixty now and Mum only worked part-time. Who wants to be struggling up and down hills with shopping when you can walk round the corner on the nice flat road to the local shop?

I didn't mind Kendal; there are far worse places in the world to be. It was a big town and had plenty going on, including a large library, and a few big shops on the high street. My heart, though, belonged to Ambleside. I liked being able to hear the birds in the morning, I liked the familiarity of the local people, the way that the postmen would leave your packages in a safe place if you weren't in, and the fact you could be completely in the middle of nowhere in a matter of minutes. Soon, I'd have to start looking for somewhere to live, start trawling through the Westmorland Gazette for places that might be suitable. The waiting list for council houses was so ridiculously long that you practically had to be living in a doorway to be offered a house within a relatively short time frame. It was a huge problem for the area, and there was no doubt that it would be much harder than finding somewhere in Manchester, because everyone likes the idea of living in the Lake District.

It's another week before I start working at the Westmorland General Hospital. My midwifery short program is due to start after I've had the new baby, and I think that I'll have a fair shot at starting it with a little one in tow. Mum and Dad have said they'll help. There are grants available for people like me - single parents. The baby can go to nursery a couple of days a week. It won't be forever, just until we are sorted. Just until we find our feet.

House hunting became my main task, and I applied for houses in Ambleside that were listed with agencies that focus on affordable homes for local people - National Trust properties – or anything else that was going. My friend, Hannah, came with me to look around a couple of little cottages with high ceilings and high rents to match, and a couple of modern looking houses with rent so expensive that I wondered how it could really be classed as an 'affordable' rent for local people. It was a growing problem in the Lakes and it had been for years – I was well aware of it. It was why so many young people left the area because you couldn't buy a garden shed in Ambleside for the amount of money a house would cost elsewhere.

Eventually, I was offered a house on the road that runs from Ambleside to Rydal. The locals know it as the 'Under Loughrigg' road and it's usually full of tourists heading to or from the major tourist destinations, or locals taking a short-cut from the ridiculous traffic that builds up on the A591 in the summer months.

I would be able to walk to the stepping-stones easily from our house, and the walk into the village would be a little way with a pushchair, but I told myself that I would manage. I didn't have time to be picky. I didn't have the money to waste on a private rent. As much as I loved Mum and Dad, I was a grown woman with my own responsibilities. I needed my own space.

It was late winter when I eventually moved into the house – the beginning of February to be exact. The weather was bitter and I was glad to have the log burner, which provided the downstairs of the cottage with a good amount of warmth. I loved my little house, the garden, the country kitchen, and the three upstairs bedrooms. It meant that the baby could have its own room and I could still have a room spare for people to sleep in – visitors and things, friends from college.

I missed you more and more, Iris, as my pregnancy progressed. I'd arranged for a local florist to take flowers to your grave every other week. Flowers that would last. I paid her in advance and told her it was important. Just because I couldn't take you with me, didn't mean I wouldn't make sure that you were still looked after. I promised that I would come back, as often as I could.

It felt to me like you didn't belong here, that you belonged to my other life, which saddened me. It felt like, every time I mentioned you in passing, someone shuddered, or fell silent. It happened more times than you would like to think. Even the midwives were concerned about me wanting to give birth to the new baby in Kendal, which was a midwife-led maternity unit that only facilitated normal pregnancies and natural births. They were worried that after you, Iris, something bad might happen again. They wanted to cover their own backs, because I wasn't as textbook as they hoped. But I didn't want to be in a big, well-equipped hospital like I had been before. I didn't want to be surrounded by machines that would inevitably remind me of giving birth to you. I couldn't afford to break down. I couldn't afford to go through all of this, to have a beautiful, healthy baby that gets taken away from me because right now I couldn't even look after myself.

Winter turned into spring, which turned into summer. I started going back to the Sunday meetings at the Kingdom Hall in Kendal with my Mum. I started going around delivering 'Watchtower' magazines to those who wanted them. It helped a little, knowing that there were people that cared. Knowing that people with faith could help me on my journey of healing, my journey into a new life. I'd known most of the congregation for all of my life, but there were new faces now too – young families with babies and children. People who I could relate to. People who would become my friends.

I hadn't had much contact with your father during the pregnancy. To be honest, I didn't really have anything to say to him. The twenty-week scan had been normal, which was a huge relief for me. The doctors gave me a foetal heart monitor so that I could listen in if I felt worried or anxious, and it helped quite a lot. The new baby was growing well, and I finished work two months before my due date. I was much bigger than I had been when I was pregnant with you, because you'd already stretched my tummy once, while you were growing inside me. It was harder to work when people thought I was more pregnant than I really was and I was worried about what people would think of me - for having this baby on my own. There was still a stigma attached to single parents, you see. People would think badly of me, yet it was hardly entirely my fault that things had turned out this way.

When the time came for the new baby to be born, I wasn't worried or anxious. I didn't have any fears about if the new baby would be born alive or dead, like I'd had with you. This baby was going to be fine. There wasn't any need for panic.

Mum drove us to the Helme Chase Maternity Unit, the morning that I went into labour. Six hours later, she was here - your little sister, Poppy.

Chapter Thirteen

What can I say about those early times with Poppy?

Well, she wasn't like you Iris; she had dark brown hair and eyes that looked confused and startled. She wiggled around in her plastic cot, which was located at the end of my hospital bed. You were happy and restful in my arms – you didn't bother or fuss. But then, you never left the hospital, never had a chance at life, while Poppy here had it all in front of her, all hers for the taking. It didn't seem fair for you, Iris; I know that.

I spent a few days in the hospital, though I didn't really need to. It was nice to have time to enjoy Poppy. The first night, they took her into the nursery and let me have some well-earned sleep. In the hospital, all of my meals were cooked for me and the midwives were on hand. It was nice to wake up at 3am with my crying baby and be offered a cup of tea and a piece of toast. It was nice to be able to disappear for half-an-hour in the bath without having to take Poppy with me.

Mum and Dad collected us when it was time to leave. We strapped Poppy tightly in her car seat and drove back to Ambleside, more carefully, I think, than Dad had driven in a good twenty years. There were a mountain of cards and gifts that had been pushed through the letterbox, and I was amazed at the generosity of others in such dire economic times. Mum had been busy at the cottage, and had left my freezer full of meals that I only needed to reheat in the microwave. She'd baked cakes for any visitors, and had run the hoover round the whole house.

I was overwhelmed at having Poppy. Everything seemed to take twice as long, and I worried about leaving her alone while I was nipping to the toilet or putting the kettle on. Poppy was restless at nights, and life became a haze of feeding and napping in-between visitors. The health visitor called round to the house to weigh her and make sure everything was going okay, and I was told to pop in at the baby clinic to have her weighed every other Thursday, which ran in the village library.

My friends were in their late-twenties now. Some of them had settled down and married, but there weren't many babies around. Most of them had focused on their careers and lived for month-long holidays where they didn't have to worry about children. But for me, Iris, I loved being a mother. I took Poppy out in her pushchair every afternoon for a walk round the park, or a trip to feed the ducks and we went to baby swimming at a local leisure club. I liked coming home and making meals; I liked people commenting on how well we looked. But that isn't to say that it wasn't a difficult, emotional time too.

I hadn't spoken to Joe since I'd had Poppy. I'd heard that he was with someone else now, another woman. I tried hard not to feel bitter and resentful, tried hard to focus on what I had. He wasn't interested in your sister. At first, I thought that he didn't want to know her in case she was ill, in case he formed an attachment to another child that was going to be taken from him. But, as time went by, I began to realise that some people just aren't cut out to be parents. They are too selfish - consumed by living their own lives in which they can put themselves first and pretend that their child doesn't exist.

In the end, I stopped calling and texting him to come and see Poppy. What was the point? He clearly wasn't interested. He'd nod at all the right places, but he didn't really want to know his daughter. He shunned my suggestions of taking her out by himself, of me leaving him with her so that they could have some real, quality father-daughter time. It hadn't even crossed his mind that I might want a break, that I was looking after Poppy by myself twenty-four hours a day and seven days a week. His time was too precious to be wasted on his daughter. I didn't need him anymore. I wasn't that needy young woman who needed everything to turn out right, even if it never would. More to the point, I didn't really want anything to do with a man that could put his own needs in front of the needs of his child. I phoned the Child Support Agency so that Poppy would get what she was entitled to – financially, at least, but that was it. From that day on it was Poppy and I against the world.

We were busy with life, Iris. I brought Poppy to visit your grave, but she was far too young to understand it. I went back to work to complete my midwifery short program and Mum and Dad took care of Poppy one evening and one day a week, and she went to the local nursery another two days. I thought that it was important for her to mix with other local children her age - the children that she would grow up with, go to school with. Beth, a friend I made at the local toddler group, sent her little boy there too. I felt bad about leaving Poppy, but lots of parents go out to work. I wanted her to understand the value of money, to understand that life was better for people who contributed to society. I didn't have anything against people who couldn't work, or who chose not to while their children were very small, but I wanted better things for us. I wanted holidays in the sun and a car that was reliable, and I was far too proud to ask for even a penny from my own parents, even though they would have willingly given it to me.

So, our lives had a new pattern. We didn't forget you as we moved forward, though I began to talk about you to others less and less. I think that it's such a taboo subject, that people like to keep things like this behind closed doors. I don't know why, though, because I felt that I had nothing to hide. An ink footprint of yours hung in a frame in our living room. I was stronger now. I could talk about what you were like, how awful it was losing you. I would rather people asked me questions to my face than talked about me behind my back. Beth had told me that another woman at the toddler group had told other women that I'd had you because I 'didn't believe' in abortions because I was a Witness. While the latter may be true of most Witnesses, it didn't influence my own decision. I had you because it was the right thing to do for us. And until they had been in that situation themselves, then how would they know how they would react and what choices they would make?

Poppy grew into a happy toddler. We were happy with life, happy bundling along. I finished my midwifery short program and was lucky to get a job based in Kendal. My new working hours consisted of a full day in a busy GP clinic on Mondays and a Tuesday daytime and a Thursday night shift at the hospital. It suited us well. I took Poppy on holidays in the sun; I bought a new car and a few hens for our garden. You'd have been pleased with me, Iris. Pleased at how we were all moving on.

Just before Poppy's second birthday, I met a man in a supermarket one Friday afternoon. Quite quickly, we became more than friends. Things were changing for us and life was good. I was feeling much better now, Iris. I felt like I didn't need to write to tell you how things were going anymore. I felt that whatever we were doing, you were with us. So I've decided to put my paper away for now and say farewell.

It's not goodbye, because you'll never be gone to me. I'll make sure that Poppy knows all about you. I'll always miss you, Iris. Take care.

PART TWO

Chapter Fourteen

<u>Mary</u>

When I was a little girl, I used to dream of being a mother. I had this doll, Annie, who I used to keep wrapped in an old blanket, and I carried everywhere. When I was old enough to be a mother and the children didn't come, I didn't feel sad or depressed. I didn't feel bitter or resentful. I didn't think that what we needed to do was to endure lots of unnecessary tests, hormone therapy, and then the inevitable IVF. Instead, what I believed was that Bob and I had a different purpose in our lives - we would find our family through adopting children. It didn't matter if the children we loved had grown inside another woman. All that mattered was that they had a loving home, with us.

Over the years, since we adopted the girls, I have wondered many times: what makes a good mother? Is flesh and blood really all that important in today's modern world? Or is it irrelevant? Is it really all about providing the things that children need and picking them up when they fall?

Emma and Sophie came to be with us so easily. We hadn't long since endured all the long interviews with Social Services to make sure that we would be 'good parents'. I had cringed when they wanted to look through our bank statements and talk to our neighbours. Bob had shrugged it all off because things like that didn't matter to him. He said he had nothing to hide and nothing to be afraid of. That the right children would come to us when the time was right.

I remember casually telling the woman who was preparing our adoption case that we were Jehovah's Witnesses, over coffee, in one of those 'getting to know you' interviews. It was the mid-1980s and back then things were different, people were less tolerant to anything that most people didn't think was normal. I was worried as the social worker wrote something down on her notepad when I had told her. She frowned and her mannerisms towards us changed.

It came from nowhere, but I felt the need to put her right about us. I couldn't have her labelling us as religious fanatics. Couldn't let her be the reason that would stop children from having a good, loving home with us. I remember, so clearly, the words that I spoke to her on that afternoon:

"Bob and I are just normal people. We do normal things; we have normal jobs. I know you might think that we are strange, that maybe even people like us shouldn't be given children. But we would love any child that came to us with our whole hearts. We would care for them, protect them, and shower them with love. We don't drink; we've never taken drugs. We pay all our bills on time. We are respectable people, and before you write us off as 'new-age hippies' or people who follow some kind of strange cult, perhaps you should learn a little respect for other peoples' beliefs and find out what being a Witness really means."

My hands were shaking as I finished speaking. Bob smiled to me behind her back. I wondered, for a moment, if perhaps I had just made a terrible mistake? The woman certainly left hastily afterwards, but less than a week later, we were approved. We celebrated with dinner in our favourite restaurant; I had the salmon, while Bob, who wasn't a vegetarian, tucked into some lamb.

We barely had time to think about what we were going to need for our children, when we got the call to say that they had two girls who were quite young that might be 'suitable' for us. We were told that the children were being looked after in a home that was full of unwanted and abandoned children which was enough to pull at anyone's heartstrings.

Even now, nearly thirty years later, I wished that we could have taken them all, that we had a large enough house, and enough money, to care for all those little children, who were so tiny and so helpless. It shocked me that places like that still existed. They refrained from calling it an orphanage, since they were going through the process of closing them down all over the country, and instead called the building a 'care home.' The home was split into different sections – one section for girls and another for boys and then there was a further division between children who were up for adoption and the children who were to be fostered.

When we walked into the main hall, the two girls sat together - apart from the other children. The people in charge of the home didn't tell us why they were there, just that they had witnessed some terrible things. They didn't elaborate any further and I didn't dare to ask them anything else. We would face whatever troubles the girls would have together, as a family. Where they came from didn't matter to us, only where they were going to.

Emma was four-years-old and Sophie just over a year. I was certain they would have no trouble getting a new family for Sophie because she was very young - young enough to forget her troubled past if she hadn't already. But things were changing for children who were looked after by the state and they wanted to keep siblings together wherever it was possible. They told us that Emma wouldn't let Sophie out of her sight; that they'd had to move them into a room together at night time, because there was no other way they could control Sophie's sobs, which would otherwise just grow louder, and louder. It was just heartbreaking. They wanted the girls to have a quiet, stable life where they were the only children, where they could simply be themselves without having to worry about whatever had happened to them before.

At that time in our lives, Bob had been offered a new job in the North of England as a hotel manager and we had decided to relocate to the Lake District. We didn't have any ties there, so we could - quite simply - present the girls to others as our own flesh and blood. I didn't want to be deceitful to our new friends and neighbours, but Bob thought that it was best for the girls. He promised me that, as they grew older, we would begin to tell them about their biological parents - that we wouldn't keep secrets. We are not secretive people and that isn't what we would have wanted. We certainly didn't want the adoption to be a shock to them at an age where they couldn't understand and we didn't want the girls to lash out at us during their teen years for hiding the truth from them.

The woman in charge of the care home told us that we could visit the girls every day until all the paperwork was drawn up. She assured us that they would apply for special dispensation to have the adoption hurried through the courts because of our impending move up north. I tried not to think about the girls' other parents, about the life they had lived and what may or may not have happened to them. We could only take them and treat them like our own, move forward and not look back.

As I'm looking at my beautiful daughter now, lying in a hospital bed, some thirty years later, all those unanswered questions I once had begin to come back to me.

Where did Emma really come from? Who were her parents and what had they done to have their two little girls taken from them? Was Emma's accident really what the police believed it to be – no more than a drunk driver who had knocked her down and just kept on going? Or was there someone out there who, for a reason unknown to us, wanted to hurt our daughter?

In all these years that had passed by, no loving biological parents had ever appeared on our doorstep, although I had often thought (and hoped for the girls) that they would. We hadn't made things difficult; we hadn't moved around a lot or kept the girls out of the limelight. I was sure that if someone had wanted to find them, they could have done so fairly easily.

Sophie had tried to trace their parents once, when she was eighteen, to no avail. She'd wanted to know why they had been in the care home, what had happened to make them eligible for adoption. Sophie loved us and saw us as her parents, but I understood that she still had questions that needed answers. It was nothing personal; it wasn't an attack on us. Just a need to know where she had come from. I had a strong relationship with both of my daughters. I knew that no one could come between us.

Bob has always had a theory that the girls' real parents had died before we even came to have them, because who could give up such beautiful children? Who could walk away and never look back?

Although his reasoning had some logic, I wasn't so sure.

Still, why would someone want to track down a child that was only four-years-old when she was adopted? It had been nearly thirty years since the day that the girls had become legally ours. What had their parents done? Had it been so bad that, one day, someone would come and try to make it right by lashing out at their daughter? If so, why Emma? Would they come for Sophie next? Would they stop there, or would they go after Emma's children? Were we all really safe, or were we all unbeknown to ourselves, walking on very thin ice?

I left my lifeless daughter in the ICU, turned on my mobile phone, and called the one person that

I thought would be able to help us: Bob's old school friend, now turned private detective, Edward Harper.

It was time for answers to the questions we had never dared to ask. It was time for the truth.

Chapter Fifteen

__Edd__

Life in Cumwhinton, South East of Carlisle, Cumbria, was slow and steady. It was a pace that I found I rather liked. Although the population might be seen as a bit ageing for a middle-aged couple, I felt that Sarah and I were fitting in well with the die-hard locals after only living here for a few years. We were close enough for Sarah to be able to drive to work in the care home, yet still close enough to the city centre, and close enough to the M6 if we ever felt the urge to go somewhere else. There was a little shop that I could walk to every morning for my paper. What more could we really hope for?

I still worked a little - odds and ends, really, these days. It had been nearly seven years since I found Grace Winters, though, I now think of her as Chloe Sumner. I've kept in touch with Alice over the years though invariably over time things do change. Chloe was based in California these days, studying Marine biology, like Alice once had many years ago.

Finding Chloe had allowed me to become financially secure, to take time off to be with my family. I had done a lot of TV interviews in the days after she was found, it had caused a bit of a media stir, and people wanted the real facts. I even wrote a book about it all – can you believe?

I chose to work now because I enjoyed it, not because I had to. I'd done nothing on the same kind of scale since then, but that didn't matter to me. It wasn't all about the big cases - they took up a lot of my time and energy and I wasn't a glory seeker; I didn't really want all the media attention that came with it. I liked living the quiet life.

My brother, Alan, lives at the other side of the village and I like being able to pop by for a cup of tea. I also liked being able to do things when I want to - without having to worry about finishing off a job, or just doing a bit more research. That was one of the downsides to the Grace Winters case. I'd done an awful lot of travelling, and I'd spent an awful lot of time working away from home, which was fine when I was alone, but I had Sarah to think about now too.

I was in the garden on the afternoon that the phone rang. More often than not, these days, I would let the phone go straight to voicemail. Most of the calls are usually telemarketers, though I'm not sure how, since we have always been ex-directory. I was in a good mood, so I answered the phone on the fifth ring, taking it out into the garden with me, where I sat with my cup of coffee overlooking the fish swimming around in the pond.

"Hello?" I said.

"Is that Edd?" A voice that seemed familiar asked me.

"Yes..."

"It's Mary Evans, Bob's wife." she said, waiting for me to recognise and place her in my life, which didn't take me too long. Bob had been one of my childhood friends as a little boy when I was at primary school over in the northeast. I didn't have many friends as a young lad, so it wasn't hard to recall who she was. Bob and Mary had married and subsequently moved from the northeast when I was working in the police force - in my twenties. They had two little girls and ended up living in the Central Lakes for many years, but now they lived just outside of it - down the M6 a few junctions away from Cumwhinton, in Kendal.

"Mary! How are things? Is Bob still playing golf? We must get together for a round or two soon. How are the grandchildren, keeping you busy?" I asked her. Mary paused. It was the kind of pause that I didn't like to hear. The kind of pause that usually occurred before the bearer dropped some kind of bombshell.

"The grandchildren are fine, Edd, but I'm afraid there's some bad news about Emma..." she let her voice trail off for a moment, before filling me in on all the details of her eldest daughter's accident.

"Mary, that's awful...What can I do to help?" I asked her.

Emma had always seemed like a nice little girl when I'd met her over the years. She'd grown into a lovely woman, kind and considerate, and now had a family of her own – two girls and a boy. It's what I would expect though, really, from a child of

Mary and Bob. They were two of the kindest people I had ever met.

"You do remember that Emma and Sophie were adopted?" she asked me.

I was one of the few people who knew the truth. I had kept in touch with Bob when they had moved down to Cheshire and you couldn't suddenly have two children at the drop of a hat, could you? Emma was a little bit older than Sophie, I seemed to remember, but Sophie was very young, still in nappies and drinking from a bottle when the girls came to be with Bob and Mary.

"Of course," I replied

"Well, I've always had an uneasy feeling about it - the adoption, that is. Bob, of course, says that I'm being ridiculous. But we weren't told anything about where they had come from, about their lives before us..."

"It's more common than you think though, Mary, in old adoption cases. It isn't what it is now - all honest and open. People didn't know what they were getting when they took on other people's children. Important facts were hidden, because they thought that it might put people off adoption altogether. It wasn't what they wanted when they had so many children who were desperate for new homes..."

"I know. I can understand it. That home was brimming full of children and there was hardly a queue of adults waiting outside to take them home and love them. I tried to find out once, who their biological parents had been, but I got nowhere. Sophie tried, when she was eighteen, to trace her birth parents. I thought she might have had better luck than I'd had, but again, she came to a load of dead-ends. I just can't help *feeling* that knowing something about the girls' biological parents might help us now. That it might be something to do with why Emma is lying in that hospital bed. Of course, I could be wrong, but again, it just feels..."

"It feels like if it is something that will help Emma now, then it's something that you've got to do?" I filled in for her.

"Exactly," she replied.

It didn't take a rocket scientist to realise that what Mary was asking for was my help. She knew if she had any chance of tracing Emma and Sophie's biological parents, then she needed people who knew what they were doing. People who knew how to ask the right people the right kind of questions. People who were more careful and yet more thorough in their approach.

I had a sense that my slow and steady life was going to be disrupted, that we were on the verge of something big, something that could end up taking up a fair amount of both my time and resources. But Bob was my oldest friend. I had fond memories of playing football with him on Sunday afternoons - particularly in the days after Alan had gone missing, when the other children could be particularly unkind. Who wants to be friends with a boy whose brother was presumed murdered? Bob had helped me then, more than he could ever know.

"Get out anything you have on the adoption; notes, papers, phone numbers, and photographs. Names of all the people you spoke to – who was in charge of the adoption, who did the home visits, and who was there when you had contact with the girls before you brought them home. I'll be there first thing in the morning."

I went upstairs and began to pack.

Chapter Sixteen

Hannah

In all of my life, so far, I have never known real tragedy first-hand. Bad things didn't happen here. Bad things don't happen to people that I know, they happen to strangers, who live in big anonymous cities. They didn't happen here.

Ambleside is a quiet little place, where people look out for each other. Community spirit. There didn't seem to be much left in other parts of the world - neighbours murdering neighbours, people who wouldn't dare to knock next door to borrow a pint of milk, or a spoon of sugar.

Petty theft of bicycles seems to peak in the tourist seasons, but that was mostly all that seemed to happen in Ambleside. There had only been one murder on record as far as I knew, and that had happened years ago, when I was a little girl. I couldn't remember the specific details, but was sure that the murderer had been caught and faced a lengthy prison sentence.

Emma's accident has forced me to re-evaluate my own life. To look at every little angle and ask myself *am I happy?* Or, *is this really what I want?* Emma's accident has made me realise that life could just be taken in a moment, so unexpectedly.

For several years now, I've worked from nine until five at the only travel agents in the village. It's a small building, in the middle of the village, and there aren't many of us who work there – a couple of full-timers and a couple of girls with small children who job-share.

You would think that booking people's holidays would be fun and exciting - trips to the Great Wall of China, or flights to Australia to swim in the Great Barrier Reef. The reality, though, was rather different. Most people, my regulars, came in one or twice a year. They booked the *same* holidays, time and time again. The Canaries mostly, because they were warm and familiar, and they could go and get a Sunday lunch with real Bisto gravy at the English bar around the corner. One or two dared to venture further – Greece, or perhaps even Morocco.

Let me tell you, there is nothing more depressing than booking holiday after holiday, smiling happily to the customers, when you're stuck in the rainy, old Lake District. Now I wondered about packing it all in, buying a camper van, and travelling the world. My parents would say that I was having a mid-life crisis. But I don't want to look at any more pictures of the Great Wall of China. I want to go there myself, touch it, and feel it. Life is for living, isn't it?

Then, of course, there was Jim.

There was nothing wrong with Jim - not physically or mentally, at least. We had been together for so long now that I could guess what he was about to say before he said it. That I didn't even notice the little things that annoyed me. Jim worked away for months on end, on the oilrigs. He would come home for a while, get under my feet, and make a mess everywhere. We would argue and we would shout at each other for most of the time. In fact, the last few times he had been on leave, it had been a relief for us both when he actually went back to work.

I had a niggling feeling that life with Jim was all wrong, that we didn't have a healthy adult relationship. I couldn't remember the last time he bought me flowers, or told me he loved me. I think that, really, we just wanted different things in life. We argued about getting married, about how many people we would have at the ceremony. In fact, we argued so much about the non-existent wedding, it was unlikely to ever happen. Jim wanted an all singing and dancing affair, with every cousin from every far-flung corner of the globe. I was perfectly happy with a quick twenty minutes in the registry office and a slap-up meal for immediate family only in Wetherspoons.

I found myself at James's and Emma's house more often than not since Emma was taken into the hospital. At least *there*, I was appreciated and valued. I felt like I was helping out, doing a good deed to people who clearly needed it.

James was looking tired and weak, which was understandable really – there were a lot of things going on in his world – a lot of things to take in and juggle all at once. Emma's Mum, Mary, was there quite often too, and it was a relief for me to be able to talk to her about Emma's condition, about how she was really doing. I visited as often as I could, but the doctors wouldn't tell me anything. I wasn't family, see, so I didn't matter to them. It was as if twenty-five years of friendship meant nothing.

The children were always happy to see me when I turned up to do my bit. Little smiling faces would come running as I opened the door. Children were yet another thing Jim and I didn't see eye to eye on, which is why we had never had any of our own. Another thing to put on the ever-expanding list of reasons that Jim and I weren't right for each other.

Today was Thursday. Jim had been home from work for two days, and he was filling the house with his presence as he usually did – clothes littered around the house like he was a teenager, unwashed plates on the side of the sink. He didn't have anything to do every day, so quite why he didn't at least tidy up and run a hoover round was beyond me.

"I thought we'd go out for tea? The new Thai restaurant? I wandered past this morning, and the menu looks good. It's cheaper before seven, so if you get a move on..." Jim stated.

I stared at him in dumb-founded amazement. He really hadn't listened to a word I'd told him this morning, as I was getting ready for work.

"I can't, I'm going over to look after the children. Mary's going to Preston for night time visiting, and James has a work meeting in Lancaster, so he won't be back until late."

"Shall we get take-away there then? Bottle of wine? Sit by that nice wood burner of theirs with a DVD?" he asked me.

His insensitivity annoyed me.

"Jim...I'd rather just go by myself. The children will be uneasy with you around; they barely know you. You being there isn't going to be helpful..."

"Of course, it's the children you're rushing to help, isn't it, not James?" he said, accusingly. Jim stared at me; his dark eyes seemed almost black in the dim winter's light. I could hardly believe what he was saying to me. I could hardly believe that he thought that I was that kind of person, that me being round at James's meant more than simply helping out with the children.

"What's happened to us?" I whispered. Jim shrugged, and went to grab another beer from the fridge.

"In case you hadn't noticed, my best friend is very ill. Things are difficult at the moment, and you know that. You being like this..."

"Yeah you're right, maybe I should just leave?" he challenged me, expecting me to beg him to stay, expecting me to fall at his feet in tears, to tell him how sorry I was for rushing to help Emma's children when they really needed it, instead of staying at home to eat a take-away with him.

But, for once, I didn't do any of those things. I was done with a relationship that wasn't going anywhere. I was done with feeling worthless. Done with feeling that everything I did was wrong.

"Maybe you should," I replied, and walked straight out the front door without looking back.

Chapter Seventeen

<u>James</u>

It's been eleven days now since Emma's accident.

How can I begin to explain how my world has changed?

I've gone from being the full-time working Dad of three to a full-time parent and carer, juggling three small children with the endless trips to and from Preston Hospital. I know that I'm burning the candle at both ends. I know that I should be trying to take things a little easier. I'm permanently exhausted, I'm not eating proper meals, and I'm relying on other people to keep my family together.

During this time in my life, I'm beginning to realise what it would be like to be a tightrope walker. It's as if I'm balancing on a rope that is so small, so delicate. One wrong move and I'm going to come completely crashing down. The trouble is, that I can't do that. I can't afford to come crashing down. There are too many people relying on me to make this right. Most importantly, who would look after the children then?

I've called Jean Witton's husband and arranged to meet him for a coffee. I'm not sure really, what I'll say to him, but if Emma thought that Jean's death was suspicious, then it was something that I really had to consider. It was likely that she had told her husband something about baby Iris. It was likely that there were questions that needed asking; about the care that Iris had received in the hospital if Jean's suspicions had been right. It was another thing to keep me wondering late into the night.

I've also written a detailed list of all the people we know – names, dates of birth, how we came to know them, what they did for work. It's not very likely that a stranger knocked Emma down, although, it was always another possibility to explore.

In the last two days, I've been calling all of these people, finding out where they were on Monday evening, making sure that someone else can verify their information. I'm beginning to realise how difficult it is to be a detective. You can't just take someone's word for it, even if they have known Emma for most of her life. Even if I would trust them with my children. The investigation would come crashing down if just one little detail was wrong - or overlooked. There were five people in Emma's phonebook that I couldn't get hold of at all. I know it doesn't seem like a lot, but what if one of them holds the key to solving all of this mystery?

Often, late at night staring up at the ceiling, I've wondered what I'll do when I do find out who knocked down my wife. My instinct tells me that I should beat them to a pulp, give them what they deserve. I'm not a violent person, but for once in my life, I feel like I could be. That hitting someone hard in the face would make me feel much better. It isn't what Emma would want though. She's never liked violence, never even tapped the children on the back of their hands for misbehaving. Emma would say that violence didn't solve anything. Maybe she was right.

Finding the folder had marked a turning point for me. It gave me the conviction that what I was doing was right. I'd found it hard to understand what Emma had been through without me, and I wondered why she didn't think she could talk to me about it.

I'd phoned Joe and given him a very large piece of my mind, which, of course didn't really solve anything. I had always thought that he was mad to have such disinterest in Poppy – not wanting to come to the school plays, the ballet shows. Poppy was lucky if she was remembered on her birthdays or at Christmas. We'd taken to removing any gift tags from items he would remember to send, which were few and far between, because it seemed cruel. It's was like saying to her *this is from your Daddy, but he doesn't want to see you.* How can you say that to a little girl? How can you let a child grow up thinking that they are unloved?

It made my skin crawl that Joe and Rebecca *suddenly* wanted Poppy. That I could be forced to hand her over to them every other weekend, every school holiday. Their solicitor had gone so far in saying that Poppy had no place with us with Emma being in the hospital, that they had every right to seek full custody. It made me angry. Just who did they think they were?

I'd walked into the village to hand a letter about their ridiculous proposals over to my solicitor, who agreed that things didn't look good. But he told me not to worry, because they didn't have a contact order - we could force them to undergo parenting assessments and supervised contacts. Joe simply couldn't come to our house and demand his daughter. It should have made me feel a little easier about the whole situation, but it didn't. I worried about them turning up at the school gates to collect Poppy from school. Joe's name was on her birth certificate. He had rights. The school wouldn't turn him away unless I had a residency order stating that Poppy legally lived with us, which I didn't. The head teacher had tried to look sympathetic when she told me this news. I then had to resolve to make sure that someone was there to collect Poppy ten minutes before home time. That Poppy was always the last one dropped off and the first one collected. It was all becoming a living nightmare.

Hannah was coming over this evening. I was supposed to be going off to a work meeting in Lancaster, a meeting that had been long planned and that I really had to attend, but luckily, it had been cancelled at the last minute. I decided that it would be good to have Hannah over for a drink, to talk about what she thinks Emma would want me to do. So I hadn't told her about the cancelled meeting. Jim was home from working away and I sensed that things weren't good between them. In the past few days, Hannah had spent more time looking after my children than with her partner, but she didn't seem the least bit worried. In fact, she seemed more than willing to drop her entire life for us.

I realised that I had underestimated Hannah's capabilities as a friend. Despite her somewhat ditsy nature, it seemed that she would go above and beyond to help anyone in any way that she could. I would be eternally grateful to her for helping me out, for making the children's lives more normal. She'd insisted on taking all three children to the local zoo, and I was quietly relieved because it would have been too much for me. We went to the zoo on a regular basis with Emma. I found the children's recollections of their mother painful, but I didn't want to stamp them down, I didn't want to make them feel that talking about her was forbidden.

Hannah arrived flustered. She let herself in and went straight to retrieve a glass for the bottle of red wine she had under her arm.

"It's a bit cold I'm afraid; it's like the arctic circle out there," she said, pouring her glass near full.

"Everything okay?" I asked her. She seemed on-edge. More uneasy than usual.

"I told Jim to leave." She replied taking a large gulp of her wine and pulling a bar of chocolate from her handbag.

"I'm sorry..." I said. I wasn't sure exactly what to say. Jim had seemed all right the few times I'd met him over the years, the few times that the four of us had gone out together, but I'd often wondered how they clicked. Hannah and Jim were very different, personality wise. I got the impression that Jim liked to come across as nice and friendly, but that he was probably not pulling his weight in their relationship. Emma and I had been lucky.

"It's been a long time coming, really. Emma thought he was useless. Now that she's not here...I feel...well, I feel like I should be taking control of my life," she continued assertively. Only Hannah could take something negative and turn it into a positive. I admired her inner strength.

I told Hannah about the cancelled meeting, grabbed another glass, poured myself a glass of red, and joined her on the sofa. As the children slept, we talked for hours about our memories of Emma, about the funny situations that we had found ourselves in with her over the years. We opened another bottle of red. We talked about what we should do for her, what she would want. It felt good to be able to talk to someone who knew her so intimately. To be able to talk, without holding back my fears about what abstaining from the blood transfusions really meant.

"So, about Jim. He's still going to be there when you get back, isn't he?" I asked her.

"Don't remind me...," she said, exasperatingly.

"Stay here...No really, I mean it. It'd be nice to have adult company around and the children love you. It'd be a big help having you around," I told her.

"Are you sure? You've got so much going on already; you don't need to add this to your pile of worries."

"It's a purely selfish motive, I assure you. Plus, I need an excuse to stop my mother and mother-in-law from being here as much as they are. They're beginning to drive me round the twist." I managed a weak smile.

"Thank you," she said, smiling back.

If only I could have known that having Hannah here would eventually make things even worse.

Chapter Eighteen

<u>Mary</u>

Edd arrived at precisely nine o'clock the following morning. Bob laughed at his predictability - Edd was always on time for everything. He carried with him a small holdall and placed it down in the hallway, before joining us in the kitchen.

Though Bob and Edd met on a fairly regular basis, I hadn't seen Edd in over a year. He looked like he had aged, but well. He seemed happier these days, more at peace. Bob said that he had never seen Edd so grounded in all the years that he had known him. That Edd had always been a restless soul. I was pleased that he had managed to make a new life with Sarah and that finding Alan had allowed him to become his happier self.

I could tell Edd was eager to go through all of the papers, to talk about our concerns about Emma. I made a fresh pot of tea and carried it to the kitchen table. Edd started looking at the papers - the adoption certificate, and the change of name deeds. There weren't half as many papers as I seemed to remember and they didn't seem to tell us anything revolutionary. Still, that was Edd's job. I was sure that if anyone could find them, he was the man.

When Bob went out to get his morning paper, I decided that now was a good time to air yet another of my worries about Emma to Edd. I really needed him to consider all of the angles.

There had been something that had concerned me more than it had concerned Bob over the years. Bob didn't care much about what other people thought about him or his family; he said that he only had to answer to himself, and Jehovah. I often wished that I could have been similar.

"Edd, I think there's something else that you may want to consider..." I began. Edd looked up at me, attentively.

"It's just that I know that many people don't like Jehovah's Witnesses. More than that, I'd go so far as saying that many people really hate us. You know, I've lost count of the number of times people have hurled abusive words at me or slammed a door in my face." Edd looked at me - compassionately.

"Why do you think that is, Mary?" he asked me. I thought about it for a moment.

"I don't really know but I think that a lot of people are misinformed about us. They seem to think that we are in some kind of secret cult. They don't know that all our meetings at the Kingdom Hall are, in fact, open and that anyone is welcome to join us at any time. The big thing, I think, is that they don't understand our reasons for abstaining from blood. It comes from a direct bible quote - a message straight from Jehovah. They think that we are happy to just let people die, children. They don't know that there are other ways, other means, of keeping people alive. Blood isn't always as necessary as people think. Jesus foretold that we would be hated by others on account of his name. I know that. But real hatred towards others can be such a terrible thing."

Edd looked at me, confused. I could see that he thought I was being irrational - that I was thinking that someone out there could hate Witnesses so much that they would do something like this. I sincerely hoped that he was right.

"You know, Mary. I've known you and Bob for a long time. I'm not a Witness, and you know that. But I do believe that you are thoughtful and kind people. That you help others. That you would do anything to help other people, and I don't just mean your brothers and sisters from the Kingdom Hall – I mean *all* people. I understand why you don't celebrate Christmas. I can see why some people might think that it is cruel to make a young child miss celebrating such a big holiday, or not having all their friends over for a birthday party once a year. Yet, I know that your children have grown up with gifts in their lives, with nice family holidays and with more love and affection than plenty of other people show their children. What is it that makes you think you're different from other people who follow religions? Why is it that people get rattled by Jehovah's Witnesses?" he asked, curiously.

"I don't think that people like us calling, or going door to door, dropping off the Watchtower and Awake magazines. Some people will chat with us. Some of them like us to come weekly, for Bible Studies, so that they can find out more about what being a Witness means. Though these people are few and far between. I think that society is changing. People are too busy to have time for other people and everyone is encouraged to go along with what is 'normal' without questioning it."

I paused for a moment, lost in my own thoughts. I remembered when I had worked in a little cafe for a while when the girls were small. I got to know people, regulars. People who would come in for a morning coffee or a bit of cake. I got chatting with a lovely lady who lived in the village. She had small children too and I wondered, for a brief moment, if we would become friends. I didn't work in the cafe during the holidays when the girls were younger because the cost of childcare didn't seem worth it and I liked having those long summer days to enjoy my family. We didn't have the girls so that someone else could enjoy all of the best bits. But during summer, I still went out on ministry work whenever I could. By complete chance, I'd knocked on the same woman's door. She looked at me and said, without thinking, *'Oh no, you're not one of those.'* In that moment, all of those hours of talking to her in the cafe seemed futile. She'd written me off with nothing more than a bad observation. Of course, she tried to apologise, but the damage had already been done. She didn't know anything about being a Witness. I was reminded then of a famous quote by the Dalai Lama *'where ignorance is our master, there is no possibility of real peace.'*

Edd's next words broke my thoughts, and brought me back to reality.

"So you think that it's possible that Emma may have upset someone doing her..." he struggled to find the right word.

"Ministry work, we call it. Going from door to door."

"But you said that Emma had become...somewhat lapsed recently?"

"Yes, she had. But I just have this feeling. I'll look up who she used to do her bible studies with and see if any of the other brothers and sisters remember any incidents of rage or violence against her when she went calling."

"Is it possible...I wonder - do you think that the attack on Emma could have come from inside the congregation? Maybe someone out there was angry that Emma had lapsed, or that she married a non-believer?"

"No," I responded firmly. There was always one thing that had been clear in my mind about being a Witness. That we were a family.

"We have a very strong community. We take pride in looking out for each other, helping each other. Not just our group here in Kendal. There were nineteen million of us who attended the memorial each year, although, statistically, we are around eight million in total. Everywhere we go, we reach out to our brothers and sisters all over the world. We can call on them in times of hardship. We can be sure that they would be there to help us in the same way that Bob and I would throw open our doors to anyone in need of help."

Edd nodded in agreement, but I could sense that he seemed agitated by my outpour and was trying to see how this could all fit in with what had happened to Emma.

"I'm going to focus first, Mary, on the adoption. On what happened to Sophie and Emma's biological parents. If they are still alive, they shouldn't be impossible to trace. They might have answers, about why the girls were put up for adoption. Such as - why they didn't want them, or why they couldn't care for them any longer? James is certain that Emma thought she was being followed, and it makes me wonder if her other family had been looking for her - lurking in the shadows, so to speak. Once we have that information, and we can rule out them and the wider family as suspects, then we will start looking at the people that Emma knew personally; people that may have a grudge against her. People she might have upset. A list of the houses that she used to call on would be most helpful."

"I'll have it arranged as soon as I can," I told him.

Edd was a good man. Although he wasn't one of our brothers, I knew that he would do whatever he could to help us solve this mystery, to find the person who had knocked Emma down, and to allow justice to be sought. I just had to keep faith.

Chapter Nineteen

Edd

There was a surprisingly small amount of paperwork that Mary and Bob held about the adoption of their daughters in the 1980s. What they did have though, seemed to be all in order.

The girls' previous surname had been Steel. The next step was to run their names and dates of birth through a national database to try and trace the biological parents. An adoption order always overruled any predeceasing birth certificates, so sometimes even this was more difficult than it appeared. Sophie didn't get far with her own search, because the national database told her what she already knew, that they had been adopted by Mary and Bob, because Sophie didn't have the means to look deeper in the system – the ability to access the original record of her own birth.

I was going to have to call in some favours, from my time in the force, to gain access to the older records and to try to locate Mr. Steven Brann who had been in charge of the adoption. Bob told me that Sophie had spoken with Mr. Brann some years back, and apparently he had insisted that he couldn't remember any details about her birth parents and that, unfortunately, all the official documentation surrounding their adoption had been lost.

It all seemed a bit suspicious to me.

A quick internet search told me that Mr. Brann was still alive and still living in Chester, on the outskirts of the city. That he has a wife and two teenage sons. Tomorrow, I planned to drive south and find Mr. Brann for myself – to see if he was telling the truth, or if his memory could come back to him with a few gentle reminders.

I suspected some kind of foul play over the adoption, which was hurried through because the Evans family had to get up to the Lake District for Bob's new job as a hotel manager. It seemed strange though, that out of all the possible parents that could have been chosen, Mary and Bob who had planned to take the girls somewhere that they wouldn't be likely to be found, were selected. It made me wonder what had happened to them before the adoption. Why were Social Services so keen to make sure that the girls were kept out of the limelight? Why had no other potential family come forward to claim them?

I spent a couple of hours going through Mary and Bob's paperwork before lunch. Double-checking dates, cross-referencing the information to make sure it all added up. I spent quite a bit of time reading the psychological reports from the psychologist Emma had seen briefly as a child due to her night traumas. Mary and Bob had withdrawn her from the psychologist when the terrors and nightmares seemed to reduce, though the psychologist had come to no firm conclusions as to why they were occurring or what the root of Emma's problems may be. I had strong suspicions that they had something to do with an event that Emma may have witnessed as a child. An event that had been hushed up by the authorities in charge of the adoption. An event that Mary and Bob knew nothing about.

The most obvious answer, in my mind, would be domestic violence at its worst. The children did not seem physically harmed when they were adopted, but that didn't mean that the children couldn't have been exposed to Daddy beating Mummy on a regular basis for years before. Or, it could have been a case of severe negligence - child cruelty. Yet, the children didn't seem to have any problems dealing with adults, and there were certainly no problems in them accepting Mary and Bob. Mary told me that she almost expected Emma to ask her about her biological parents one day, but she never did. The real question was – why not?

I needed to talk to Sophie and James before I headed to Chester for answers. Sophie had been just over a year old when the adoption had taken place, so it was highly unlikely that she had any recollection of her life before Mary and Bob. James, I thought, was in a good position to tell me if Emma still experienced sleeping problems or if she had managed to shake off the anxious feelings of her childhood. To tell me about how Emma had been recently. To elaborate on any ill feeling between her and others that might have been going on at the time she was knocked down and to ask him: who did he think was to blame? Who did he think had reason to harm his wife?

The road ahead was going to be long and uneven. I seriously doubted that this was going to be a simple, clear-cut case. I hoped that the answers would come quickly, that the Evans family could find peace in knowing the truth.

I, above all people, know that it is the not knowing that is the worst. All those years that Mam and I endured, not knowing if Alan was okay, not knowing if he was safe. All those years of wonder. People need closure to be able to move on - to draw a line and move forward with their lives.

I had to do whatever I could to make that happen.

I picked up my mobile, and started to make some calls.

Chapter Twenty

<u>Sophie</u>

What is your earliest memory? Being pushed on the swings? Learning to ride a bike? Your first trip on a plane? Your first day at school?

I've tried really hard over the years to erase my first real memory. Why? Because it's a memory that doesn't make sense. It's a memory of being trapped, of the walls sinking in on me. I've always hated small places. Lifts and train toilets are the worst. Mum and Dad told me that I've never been trapped anywhere before. That I've never been locked in a toilet, or a shed. That's why my memory has never made sense. The recurring memory of helplessness. The memory that Emma is in charge, Emma will look after me. That I don't need to be afraid of whoever is out there.

But now, Emma is gone.

Who will look after me now?

My second memory comes much more easily to me. I was about five-years-old. Mum and Dad bought us a kitten. It was springtime, and we called the kitten Fluffy because of its white, fluffy coat. We had wanted a dog really, but Dad had said that it wasn't fair to keep a dog in the house all day long. That it would be up to Mum to look after the dog while we were at school and he was at work all day - she had enough jobs to do as it was.

Emma and I used to torment Fluffy - following her around the house, putting her in a dolls pram, and pushing her around in it in the garden. One day, some months later, little Fluffy went missing. Emma and I were distraught. We made posters and put them up all over the village. Dad sat us down and told us that the reality was that we lived on a housing estate, that cars drove far too fast up the road, and he thought that Fluffy might have just taken herself off the road, quietly, to die in a bush, after being hit by a passing car. It's what cats do, he told us, when they get hurt. They like to be alone.

The next morning, I went looking with my torch under every bush on the estate. I was meticulously methodical. Eventually, I found her. Her soft, white coat was matted with blood. Fluffy was dead. I carried her home, and Emma and I wept for days. We buried her in the back garden. It was the first time that we realised that humans can be cruel and unkind which made us even sadder. At the Kingdom Hall on Sunday, we prayed silently to ourselves that Fluffy would have no more pain and suffering. That she would be sleeping, peacefully.

Some time afterwards, Dad told us that we could have another kitten, if we wanted. But the pain was too raw. We only wanted Fluffy, not a replacement. We didn't want to put another animal though any more suffering, so we declined the offer. Quite simply, I think that we knew that we couldn't face the pain of losing another animal. In fact, I've never owned an animal since because other people's actions worry me. I didn't want to have to deal with another dead animal that I loved and cared for because someone else's actions could be so cruel.

For as long as I can remember, Emma and I had known that we were adopted. To us, it was simply just one of those things. Our parents were our parents and we had no doubt that they loved us and cared for us. For me, they were the only parents that I could remember, and I hadn't known anything about my other life. Emma, though, was different. She had a vague memory of a woman with dark-brown hair and of a mysterious day when we were told to go upstairs and hide. But that was all that she could remember.

The main thing that I didn't like about being adopted when I was growing up was other people's reactions to it. In secondary school, the other kids seemed more interested in my biological parents than I was. Then, one day, in science class, we started looking at people's DNA. About how a person's genetic pool shapes us, gives us blonde hair or blue eyes, or makes us more susceptible to heart disease or cancer. It was the first time that got me thinking, suddenly, about who I was and where I had come from and suddenly, I wanted to know. Who were they? Why did they give us up?

Mum and Dad tried their best to help me trace my birth parents, but we didn't get very far. The records had been long since lost or destroyed. I should have, perhaps, felt disheartened, but instead I felt like it was a sign. A sign that I didn't need to know about my biological parents, because of the wonderful life I had now with parents who loved me. So, just like that, I forgot them.

Life carried on as normal. Well, as normal as it had been before.

Years went by, and I worked, I lived and I tried to enjoy life as much as I could.

That was, until the day that my sister was knocked down by that still unknown car and left for dead. Now, here I am waiting for Dad's old school friend, Edd, to come and talk to me about our adoption. As if, suddenly, the unknown is important once more. But our real parents can't really have anything to do with Emma's accident, can they?

The doorbell rang at just past two o'clock. I let Edd in and made a pot of tea. We chatted idly for some time, before he started getting down to the real questions: *Do you remember your parents? Did Emma ever speak about them? Is there anything strange lurking in the back of your memory?*

I answered his questions as best as I could. I could see that Edd was a little disappointed. That he had hoped to have something a bit more concrete to go on, something that might establish who our birth parents had been or what they may have done.

"Emma had a memory of a woman with brown hair," I told him. He wrote it down on a piece of loose paper.

"I've read the psychiatric report on her night terrors. I'm sure they have something to do with her life before you girls came to be with Mary and Bob." Edd added, assertively.

I'd wondered about this too myself over the years. There had been nothing out of the ordinary about our life in the Lake District. Mum and Dad were kind and gentle people who were not violent in the least.

"I have never had the night terrors, but I have always had panic attacks about being in small places, about being trapped." Edd made further notes on his paper. I wondered how significant all of this would be in the grand scheme of things? Perhaps it was irrelevant, but perhaps it was linked to the nightmares that plagued Emma as a child.

When Edd had finished with his questions, he talked about his investigation - about how he was going to try to trace our parents and about the difficulties he might have along the way.

"It is possible that the answers that I will find might not be nice. Of course, it's also equally possible that there is nothing at all wrong with your birth parents. They might have sent you away for your own safety or because they just wanted a life without children, maybe they had jobs with difficult hours, maybe they found themselves stationed overseas." I nodded, but I found that hard to believe. Firstly, they had never come looking for us in all of these years. I knew that Dad believed that they were both dead, though he had never openly admitted it to us. I didn't have any children of my own, but I couldn't imagine Emma willingly sending any of her children away even if it would guarantee that they would come to no harm. But then you never know, really, how you would react in a situation like that until you were in it – do you?

I thanked Edd for his time as I saw him off. I hoped that he would find some answers, for Mum and Dad's sake. I hoped that his investigation would mean that he could tell Emma's children that the person who had caused so much pain to our family would be accountable for their crimes. That they would be punished for ruining their mother's life.

I threw on my winter coat and gloves, picked up my handbag, and headed out towards my car. Evening visiting had become a bit of a ritual these days. I would often head over to Preston mid-afternoon and catch James before he left to come back to Ambleside. We often joked about our passing in the corridor, but it was the best thing for Emma. I didn't like to think of her lying in the hospital bed on her own, but I also knew that she wouldn't want James sitting at her bedside twenty-four hours a day, seven days a week, and that James has to do what he can to be there for their children in this difficult time.

There are ten days until Christmas.

I just hope it'll all be over by then.

Chapter Twenty One

James

     I left the hospital earlier than usual on that Friday. It was actually Friday the thirteenth, but I wasn't really a superstitious kind of person. Even if I was, then surely enough bad things had recently happened in my family. It would be *really* rotten luck for *more* bad things to come our way, especially so close to Christmas.
     Hannah finished work early on Fridays. She had offered to collect the children and take them to the indoor play area for a couple of hours. I was grateful that she could do something to let the children just be children. Everywhere I seemed to go, people seemed to think that it was appropriate to stop me in the street and ask about Emma. It was all well and good, and I was sure that they had good intentions, but it made things difficult. There were certain things that I didn't want the children to hear. Certain things that shouldn't be said at all.
     I arranged to meet Edd Harper in the pub for a pint, late that afternoon. Edd was an old school friend of Bob's and Mary had somehow enlisted his help in trying to track down Emma's biological parents. I was sceptical about how much good that would do, but I didn't want to put a dampener on Mary's elevated spirits.

Our local pub was called 'The Golden Rule.' It sat at the bottom of what the locals called 'the struggle,' which was a long, very steep, and twisty road that went over Kirkstone Pass. In the summer months, Emma would sometimes go up the pass on her mountain bike and would come back looking red-faced and flustered. But in the real winter months, the pass was usually closed, due to the hard frosts and snow.

The pub was one of the few places in the village that hadn't altered for tourists – it hadn't tried to keep up with modern times, hadn't tried to turn into something it wasn't. In winter, the roaring log fire was usually enough to entice people in. The price of bitter was reasonable, and you could order a pork pie with a bit of pickle on the side, if you suddenly found yourself peckish. People would have been up in arms about a pub like this in London.

I walked in and ordered a pint, thinking yet again how strange it was that life went on even though Emma wasn't here. People just carried on with their day-to-day tasks as if nothing un-toward was happening in the village. As if the fact there might be someone out there who was responsible for hurting Emma was irrelevant. A couple of regulars nodded and smiled my way, but I didn't stand around at the bar to chatter as I might have usually done. I went to find Edd.

Edd had tucked himself away in what was known as the back room, so I wandered quietly through there. The back room had the advantage of being a bit more private, a bit more of a place to be able to talk. He stood up and shook my hand. Edd had a good, solid, handshake. I'd googled him late last night, and his resume was impressive. Although he was well-known for finding the missing girl, Grace Winters, he'd had a string of successes in reuniting lost siblings, particularly those who had been adopted. It gave me hope that at least we might find out what Emma's biological parents had been like even if it didn't necessarily lead to anywhere.

We talked at length about Emma's dreams, about her childhood memories and her worries about being followed in the weeks before the accident. Edd didn't seem shocked by this revelation. He noted it all down meticulously. I told him about the folder that I had found, about Iris and the sudden death of Jean Witton. I hadn't told Mary and Bob about her yet because I didn't want to worry them any further, but I wanted to know what someone else thought about it all.

"Do you think it could have been a mistake? That they could have done more for Iris?" I asked Edd, cautiously.

"I'll request her medical file and take a good look at it. It's possible. It's very strange that this woman who provided the information also got knocked down by an unknown car..." Edd replied.

"I'm meeting her husband tomorrow. I'll let you know how I get on," I said.

Edd nodded.

We sat for a good couple of hours talking everything over and trying to come up with a plan for how we should move forward. In the end, we agreed that Edd would primarily focus on finding out what had happened to Emma's biological parents while I would follow up on Jean Witton. We would probably come together to make our way through the list I had been producing of the people that we knew, joined with the list that Mary was conducting of people Emma had been a regular caller to when she had been out on her ministry work. I told him that I'd managed to eliminate a few suspects, but there was still a way to go. Edd told me not to worry about the list too much for the moment, to focus on one thing at a time.

I left the pub that afternoon feeling good, feeling hopeful. Feeling that the investigations were finally going somewhere. That between us, our plans covered all the bases as thoroughly as we could given our limited resources. Together, working as a team, we could pool our information and track down who had done this to Emma.

I smiled to myself, as I swung by the Chinese restaurant next to the garage to pick up our dinner, and then drove back to the house. Things were getting better. Now, if only Emma's condition would start to improve, life would be just about perfect.

Chapter Twenty Two

Hannah

Helping James with the children seemed right. I knew that Emma would have been pleased to know that someone was looking out for her family. Taking control of the washing, running around a hoover, and making sure that the hens were cleaned out and had extra hay for this cold, wintery weather.

For once, I didn't care what Jim said or did. I ignored his pitiful texts pleading for me to return home. I let all of his phone calls go straight to answer phone. I didn't need him, or want him to be dragging me down. It was time I took control of my life. It was time that I stood back a step and looked at what was really important. It was time that I got what I deserved, someone who appreciated me for who I was, instead of someone who was insistent on belittling me about everything I did.

In our time together, Jim had always been good at moaning - the shirts hadn't been ironed, or the vacuuming hadn't been done. He would see those jobs as something extra I had to do after work, instead of something he could be doing on his leave. The trouble was that I didn't really care about things like that now. They were unimportant in the grand scheme of life. The world would carry on if the house wasn't clean or if a shirt was a little creased. Jim just didn't understand.

I took my responsibilities as the temporary, stand-in mother of Emma's children seriously. I told my boss that I would have to finish at 3pm every day to be able to pick them up from school, to try to keep them in a familiar routine. I read their reading books with them every evening, filling in the little yellow book with the appropriate comments. I talked to the teachers about how they were *really* coping. On the surface, they seemed so normal, but it didn't stop them from missing Emma. It didn't stop Millie from crying out in the night for her, or Finn asking *how much longer until Mummy comes home?*

It was James though that I was really worried about. His face was gaunt and expressionless for most of the time. He picked at the meals I cooked for him, mostly because it was impossible to eat and talk at the same time. His evenings consisted of several phone calls – usually to his parents, Emma's parents, the school, the lawyer, the social worker. There was a lot going on and there were no margins for errors.

James was due at an emergency hearing tomorrow, because Poppy's father, Joe, had suddenly, and quite mysteriously, shown a keen interest in having Poppy live with him and his wife. It was yet another thing to keep us all on edge, another thing for us to be worried about. I thought that he had a bit of a cheek, turning up after all these years. He'd certainly never been there for Poppy, and Emma had been far more tolerant in those early years than I would have been. There was something else going on with him, and I was sure that I was going to get to the bottom of it.

I managed to get hold of a number for Joe's wife, Rachel Jackson, and arranged to meet her in the village for a coffee. I knew that James wouldn't be pleased about me fraternising with the enemy, but we were left with little choice. Emma had always been so certain that Joe didn't want Poppy - that he wouldn't turn up to claim her. I knew that it was one of the reasons that James had never legally adopted Poppy. It had been such a non-issue that there was nothing in place in case this happened. This isn't what Emma would want, Poppy going anywhere within a hundred miles of Joe - so in my mind, this simply couldn't happen.

I walked to the cafe during my lunch hour. We had arranged to meet at the Apple Pie, which was a little place that was on the way out of Ambleside, towards the health centre. It seemed like a good choice because the place was always busy, even in the middle of winter. People would be too busy choosing cakes to be listening to our conversation. I found a seat towards the back, ordered a tea and a bath bun, and waited.

Rachel Jackson wasn't how I imagined she would be. Firstly, she was older. She must have a good ten years on Emma and I. Secondly, she seemed friendly as she smiled and sat down opposite me. Emma and I had discussed her over the years, and we'd always made her out to be like the ice witch from Narnia – cruel and unkind. It was hard to see how, as she looked towards me.

135

"Thank you for meeting with me," she said.

I nodded. There was no point in tiptoeing around the edges really, was there? I may as well just cut to the chase.

"I'm Emma's friend, have been for a long long time. Before Poppy, before Joe." Rachel nodded, looking a little more uneasy than she had been. I wondered if it made her nervous, if she wondered whether I knew things about her husband that she did not know.

I continued, "I've been staying with James to help him with the children because, obviously, the travel to and from Preston everyday takes up a fair amount of his time, and the investigation to determine the cause of the accident and who was the driver of the car is still ongoing."

"Yes. I know...It's very unfortunate that all of this is happening at the same time. We had tried to talk with Emma about Poppy before all of this. She refused to reply to any of our letters. Refused, point blank, for us to have any contact with her. Then, when we heard about her being in the hospital...well...Joe thought that gaining access would be *easy.* He thought that we might even have more of a chance of Poppy coming to live with us, permanently."

I took a large sip of my tea, if only to stop myself from screaming out loud that it was a completely ludicrous decision. That two strangers to a child shouldn't sit down and casually discuss her future over dinner, thinking that they knew what was best for her. Poppy wouldn't even recognise Joe if she walked past him one day in the street.

"Emma didn't tell me about any letters...." I told her, carefully.

"Yes, well, it does seem there was a lot more to Emma than what we all really thought, doesn't it Hannah?"

A long silence filled our table. I didn't want to admit that Rachel could be right, and it seemed wrong to discuss the faults of my best friend when we were in this situation - when Emma was still lying, unconscious, in her hospital bed.

"James's solicitor seems to think that you're not going to get very far with your petition for custody. That you might be given access, but it's going to take some time before you're allowed to take Poppy unsupervised," I told her, in a matter-of-fact way.

"I was hoping that you might be able to speak with him? We don't mean to cause harm or upset. But Poppy has a right to know her father."

"James *is* her father," I told her, raising my voice slightly louder than was necessary. The woman sitting at the next table glanced over.

"Poppy hasn't seen Joe for such a long time. James is the one who has been there for her, emotionally. I'm sure you can appreciate that things for Poppy are difficult enough at the moment. She's only six years old. How do you think she would feel to be ripped from her family? To be separated from her brother and sister?" I asked Rachel.

"Just because Joe hasn't seen her, doesn't mean he doesn't care."

"Really? And how has he shown Poppy he cares, in all of these years? Most years he hasn't so much as sent her a birthday card, let alone any presents."

"We knew that Poppy would never have been allowed any gifts that we sent, so, yes after a couple of years we stopped," Rachel challenged.

"Ridiculous," I told her, wondering really if Rachel was right. I certainly wouldn't have a nice thing to say about Joe to Poppy, but Emma had always been kinder. She didn't hold grudges. She always tried to let Poppy make up her own mind about her largely absent father in those first few years, before all of the contact stopped. In fact, I'd go as far as to say that Emma seemed to encourage Poppy into thinking that he was a good, kind man. I used to think that she was setting Poppy up for a rather nasty fall.

"Why now?" I asked her. Rachel paused for thought, as if wondering if she should be divulging such information to someone who could later use it against her.

"I am unable to have children of my own. Poppy is the only chance that Joe is going to have to be a father."

A slightly ironic pregnant silence filled the air between us. So much that either of us could say but no one quite daring to say it. It hung there, in the air between us. Of course, Joe was exactly the kind of man to come and claim something he thought belonged to him if he couldn't get it in any other way. I could just imagine him having a light bulb moment when he realised that he already had what they wanted, that they could easily stake a

138

claim to Poppy – whether it was in her best interests or not.

"I was happy to look into adoption, but Joe didn't want that. He said that he would find it too difficult to love someone else's child. That it wouldn't be the same. He said that we would have the best of both worlds, if we could come to a joint-custody arrangement about Poppy. We would have the benefits of having a child, but we would still be able to have time on our own. This was about six months ago, now. But as I said, Emma wasn't responsive to our communication."

I was torn between believing this stranger's tale of woe, between feeling sorry for her, being unable to have children of her own and between thinking about what the best thing was for Poppy, right here, right now. Perhaps Joe, as useless as he was, should be allowed some access to his daughter. But then access and joint-custody were totally separate things.

"James has loved Poppy as if she were his own. She is treated no differently to his own children, which of course is the way that it should be. At this moment in time, you would cause Poppy more hatred towards you by going through with your bid for custody. She is already under a lot of emotional pressure because she had such a strong relationship with Emma. You must see that?"

"I understand that it is difficult...but Joe has always provided for Poppy financially. He has always been there for her, even if she didn't know it."

"What about if I talk to James? If we can agree on some kind of access - limited access - for now?" I asked her.

"I'm afraid that won't be enough. James will see us as an enemy. We wouldn't really be included and welcomed into Poppy's life without all of this being done through the official channels."

I could see her point, but it still seemed a little heartless. It had been over four years since Joe had any contact with Poppy. Four long years of nothing. In my mind, it seemed that they had no idea about how much a child could change in four years. No idea about what Poppy liked to do, who she was friends with. No real idea about what she looked like. Did they really expect that they could come waltzing in after all of this time and expect Poppy to be happy about it? Surely just allowing her a little bit of time wouldn't make that much difference in the grand scheme of things? Couldn't they look at this again in a couple of months, at least give Poppy chance to understand what was happening with her mother, for things with Emma to be a bit more settled?

As if sensing my thoughts, Rachel began to speak again.

"Joe has been offered a job in London. We hoped that we could sort this out and that Poppy could come with us. That James could have access during weekends and school holidays..."

"I can see that Joe has not changed at all in all these years – that he still considers himself to be standing on some kind of pedestal, above all others. I would have hoped that a woman, such as yourself, might have been able to have a bit more compassion for another woman's child, instead of trying to come here and claim her as her own. Poppy is happy. She is loved. She has a good life here. I will not stand by and let all of that be taken from her, to allow her to be taken away by strangers. Trips to and from London every-other weekend. I mean, how is that ever going to work? Years ago, Emma made me Poppy's legal guardian in the event of her death. So, you see, I probably have more legal standing over Poppy than you do right now. I will not allow this. I'll spend every last penny that I have on lawyers and court cases if that is what it takes. I'll get the best child psychologists that money can buy who will tell you that Poppy will be damaged if you do this to her. You'd better tell Joe that if he wants to fight, that's exactly what'll happen. We will see what people with *real compassion* think about what is best for Poppy."

    I drew back my chair and left her sitting at the table. I walked out of the Apple Pie in such a haze of anger, that I was halfway down the street before I realised I hadn't paid for my cup of tea and cake. I smiled at the thought of getting one up on Rachel Jackson, however small it might be.

    They haven't a hope of winning, Emma, I thought, as I carried on walking back to work. I hung my coat up on the hook, sat down at my computer, and carried on working.

    I tried not to think about the conversation that I was going to have to have with James that evening. Perhaps it was time that I got my own solicitor.

Chapter Twenty Three

Edd

Talking with James had allowed me to step back and look at the whole situation surrounding Emma's accident. Already, it seemed clear that somebody out there didn't like her – or, more didn't like her looking into her past. James was going to go to Morecambe to meet with Jean Witton's husband - to find out why she had thought they could have done more for Iris, and what exactly she had seen.

After my meeting with James, I headed towards the library in Kendal. I had to go through a joining process, filling in a registration form and handing over my driving licence, which seemed a little unnecessary. But as soon as I had my library card, I was able to go into the archive room and I sat down and went through old major tabloid newspapers from the year preceding Emma and Sophie's adoption. I looked through the major headlines and the obituaries. Three women had died who had left behind two small daughters. One was murdered, one died of complications arising from a medical procedure, and the third had taken her own life by jumping off a bridge. I wrote down the names of the three women in my notepad. Was it likely that one of them could be the girls' biological mother? It was possible, and it was another avenue of enquiry that shouldn't be ruled out.

The other thing that really niggled at my conscience was the lack of paperwork surrounding the adoption, and the lack of information about Steven Brann. An ex-police friend had managed to look at the central database that the UK held on crimes. Steven Brann was not a criminal, which was almost a shame because criminals were often much easier to trace.

I had a bad feeling that something untoward went on with Steven Brann and the girls' adoption - an ulterior motive, or, perhaps even an exchange of money. Children often spent months, even years in children's homes like the one that Emma and Sophie had been in. The more that I thought about it, the more that it seemed strange that the girls were offered to Mary and Bob so soon after them being approved. They hadn't been in the children's home for long. Surely, there was a string of other children that needed to be placed in loving homes before them?

I braced myself to talk with Mary and Bob about where things would go from here. It's often harder working for someone that you care about. The lines between friendship and professionalism can become blurred. There were things about Emma and Sophie that, to me, didn't make sense. Things that I usually wouldn't have mentioned to my clients until I knew for certain, until I had some real concrete proof that my assumptions were correct. But I couldn't do that now. I wanted Mary and Bob to understand my theories. I wanted them to be able to see where I was coming from, to think about all the options, and to jog their memories. I wanted Mary to come with me to Chester, which might seem like an unusual request. I wanted her to meet Steven Brann with me, because men are often more likely to give information if they are presented with a woman like Mary. A woman who is suffering, who needs the truth in order to be able to move on with her life. A woman who needs his answers so desperately.

For the past hour, I had been preparing myself with the words I would say to Mary and Bob. I'd rehearsed them in my mind over a hundred times. Yet, when we came to sit round the table, tea pot, and cake in the middle, my mind went blank. The words I had thought of just didn't seem right, didn't seem appropriate.

I took a deep breath, and began.

"I believe that things with Emma may be more complicated than they seem. My main concern is tracing her birth parents, but there is a possibility that the threat to her life could have come from elsewhere. James found a folder of letters and documents relating to Iris. Emma had left him a letter, telling him that a woman had contacted her, out of the blue, to tell her that she thought that the hospital could have done more to save Iris. At the moment, I'm not sure if there was any element of truth in this woman's claims. Yet, in her letter to James, Emma seems convinced that this woman was not setting out for financial gain, but simply reaching out because she believed the hospital had done wrong, that Iris might still have been here if it wasn't for their negligence."

I paused for a moment, allowing them to take it all in, before continuing.

"All of this seems, perhaps, a bit farfetched, and I wondered about it myself when James was telling me about it. However, something strange happened to the woman who had been in contact with Emma. After some time considering her options, it seems that Emma had arranged to meet her - we have no idea what Emma was told, or how the meeting went. But a few days after Emma met with Jean, Jean's body was found, late one night. A passing car had knocked her down. There were no witnesses"

Once more, I let the silence fill the room. Bob looked at Mary, before he began to speak.

"We never saw her, you know, Edd - Iris. She was gone so quickly. I often wondered why the hospital seemed so keen to let nature take its course. Why they didn't have her hooked up to whatever machine could have kept her alive..." his voice trailed off, softly.

"They told Emma that Iris was too ill for organ donation. So they let her slip away, peacefully, on her own..." Mary filled in.

"James is going to meet with Jean's husband, and I've got an old friend coming to stay in Ambleside for a while. I've paid for him to stay in a bed and breakfast in the village while he is here so that he can keep an eye on Rose Cottage and to look out for people who might be watching James and the children."

"Please let us foot the bill for his expenses - whatever you need-"

"It's taken care of, Bob. Please, don't worry yourselves unnecessarily about the financial costs about the investigation. I'm here to help you. This isn't about how much money I am going to make. This is about doing the right thing for you and your family. We've been friends for a long time. I know you would do the same for me..."

"Thank you," Mary added. "We appreciate it, we really do."

I took another long sip of my tea, before bracing myself to continue. There was a question that I had to ask them, and it was a question that I was certain I already knew the answer to. Mary and Bob were simply not that kind of people.

"The adoption records are another problem. I'm going to head south to Chester for a few days. See if I can track down Steven Brann and see what he has to say about things. Just so you are both aware, I'm beginning to suspect that there were some underhand dealings to do with the girls' adoption. That things might not have been entirely legal..."

"But that's ridiculous! We have the adoption papers, we went to court. I assure you that it was all above board," Mary said, glancing sideways at Bob as she spoke.

"The legal side of the adoption, yes. But there are questions to be raised about the amount of time that both Sophie and Emma had spent in the care home. It seems so relatively short compared to other children. It just, well, it makes me wonder if there wasn't say a passing of money - to ensure that the girls got the best home, and quickly."

I looked across at both of them, and could see the shock of my accusations written all over their faces.

"Of course," I added, backtracking, "I'm not suggesting that you had anything to do with it - that you paid for your daughters. I'd find that very hard to believe. But that doesn't mean that somewhere along the line, someone else wasn't encouraging things to move a little quicker than usual..."

"We had to move north quickly because of my job. Are you saying, Edd, that us moving north might have been the perfect excuse for them? To hurry things along?" Bob asked.

"I'm saying that of all the children who were in that care home when you were approved suitable to adopt, and of all the other potential adoptive parents, well, it seems strange that two girls who had been there a matter of weeks were matched perfectly to a wonderful set of parents, such as yourselves. To people who would love the children as much as they would love their own. The fact that you were moving north could have been a large part of *why* you got the girls. If you think about it properly – if somebody wanted them to have a good life, a sheltered life, a life where they wouldn't be in the limelight..."

I watched the colour drain from their faces as the realisation hit.

"But why? Why would someone who went to such great lengths to ensure the girls had a good life. Why wouldn't they have just done all of this themselves? Why would they have just let them go? Why would they never have come back, to make sure that they were okay?" Mary asked me.

"That is exactly what I'm planning to find out."

Chapter Twenty Four

<u>Mary</u>

That evening, I packed my bags as if my whole life depended on it. I was beginning to see things in a different light. Beginning to realise that the life I thought was perfect, seemed to have major flaws in its plan.

I called James and told him about the plans, told him that Bob was around to help with the children while we were off finding Steven Brann. Edd wasn't really sure how long it would take, but hopefully no more than a couple of days. I was relieved to hear that Hannah had been helping him out with the children. Hannah had always been a good friend to Emma and the children loved having her around.

As we drove south of Kendal, joining the M6, I thought about the lives that Bob and I had when we lived in Chester. We both worked full-time then, but it was a nice time to look back on - a time when we spent more time together as a couple. Of course, I'm not complaining about the lack of time we had when the children were small. We love the girls; and we loved being parents. But they took a lot of time and energy from us in those early years and it didn't give Bob and I a lot of time on our own.

Before we adopted the girls, we lived in a small village just outside Chester called Mollington. It was a nice, little place. We had chosen to live there specifically because it felt safe. We had a large garden and the local primary school was a short walk away. Back then, we didn't know that the children would never live in this house, not for more than a few days anyway. On one of our 'getting to know you' days with Emma and Sophie, we had taken them to Chester Zoo. I remembered Emma being particularly interested in the elephants; we must have sat looking at them for hours on end. She had chosen a little soft toy elephant teddy in the zoo shop, and for years, it remained in her bedroom. It lives on a shelf in Poppy's room now.

Steven Brann, Edd told me, lived not too far from where we had lived back then in a neighbouring town called Blackon, which was considerably larger than Mollington. It was also slightly nearer to Chester city centre, and was much better served by the city buses as it ran along a major bus route. It seemed that Steven Brann still lived in the house he had bought around the time we adopted the girls. He had given up working for social services a couple of years ago, and was now semi-retired – helping his wife run her flower shop the odd day during the week. We hoped it wouldn't be too difficult to track him down.

Edd had managed to book us a couple of nights in the Holiday Inn at Chester Racecourse. The rates were reasonable and the reviews were good enough, so we went straight there to drop our luggage, grab some lunch, and come up with a plan.

While Edd collected our room keys, I went to the bar and ordered a couple of sandwiches – cheese for me and ham for Edd. I hadn't realised how hungry I was until it arrived. Meals had become a bit here and there since Emma's accident. Food isn't in the forefront of your mind during a difficult time and your life is no longer dictated by which meal comes next. Can you believe that I recently found myself nodding off to sleep in bed on a couple of evenings, when I realised that we had completely missed dinner. By then I was too tired to do anything about it, and I often awoke in the middle of the night with a rumbling tummy, I'd go downstairs and have some cereal at two or three am.

"What do you think then, Edd? Are we going in for the kill or are we going to loiter for a while?" I asked him.

Edd smiled. "You'd make a good detective you know, Mary. I thought that we would take a drive over to Blackon - find his house, survey the area, and see if it looks like anyone is about."

I nodded.

"He won't be expecting us, so hopefully he will be at home or maybe, at least, his wife," I said.

"There's a reason that I just turn up unannounced. It gives people the chance to hide from me, to pretend that I'm not around and I'm not watching. You get better results if you take them unaware."

"So you do think that Steven knows something?" I asked, hesitantly.

"I'm almost certain of it. There are just too many discrepancies. Come on, finish your tea and we will put our bags in our rooms and get going."

I took a large gulp of my remaining tea, and did just that. Less than five minutes later, we were on the road.

As we pulled into the street that Steven Brann lived on, I looked at all the houses and all the people walking along the pavement, as if there might be a hidden clue in anything. There were trees planted somewhat sporadically in people's front gardens, as if to shelter some of the passers-by from looking inside people's windows.

Edd slowed and parked his car in a street of detached houses, each almost identical in shape and size apart from the fact that some had driveways and garages and some did not. The houses formed a long, neat row.

"That one there," he said, gesturing across the road from where we had parked. "Number Fourteen."

I looked across at the house. A Ford Focus was parked in the drive. The downstairs' lights were on. I could see the faint outline of a man moving around inside. I could not see his face, but from the size of his body and my hazy memory from thirty years ago, I was fairly confident that we were looking right at Steven Brann.

"Well, no point in beating around the bush. Are you ready?" Edd asked, looking across at me. I tried not to appear nervous, or worried - but I was. I wondered if I would ever be ready to hear what

Steven Brann had to say to us. If I would ever be ready to hear the truth about my daughters.

"I'm as ready as I'll ever be," I replied, managing a soft smile.

Edd nodded. "Don't worry, I'll do the talking; this should be a breeze."

We unclipped our seatbelts, opened our car doors, and walked together up the pathway to number fourteen. Edd rang the doorbell. We waited.

Chapter Twenty Five

James

Tomorrow morning I would be driving to Morecambe to meet Jean Witton's husband for the first and hopefully the last time. I'd gone through all of the things that I needed to ask him, such as: What did she know about Iris? How could they have helped her more? Why didn't she speak out when it had happened? I also had some more sensitive questions to ask him, surrounding his wife's accident: When was she hit? Was the driver of a car charged? Why had she died?

I'll admit that I was still feeling sceptical about the whole thing, still unsure as to how this could have anything to do with Emma. I constantly had to remind myself that Emma thought that this was important, that Jean Witton was onto something, and that her death was most suspicious. It would be interesting to hear her husband's side of the events, interesting to see what he thought about this whole saga.

A more pressing issue in the last few days had been Poppy's father's insistence for contact. I'd fought it as much as I could, even the social worker agreed that now might not be a good time for Poppy. Yet, still, an order had been passed by the family courts that now allowed Joe and Rachel contact at the local contact centre – supervised -

twice a week. You might be thinking that isn't very often, that it doesn't amount to too much time, or that it isn't really a big deal. The contact centre was a thirty mile round trip. During the next few weeks, experts would write a parenting assessment on Joe and Rachel. They'd be allowed to take Poppy out, under supervision, if they wanted. In a couple of months from now we would be back in court again and it would be up to the court officials to decide how much time they would get with Poppy, and to seriously consider letting them have either joint or full custody.

My lawyer did the best he could; he was throwing every little thing he could into this: Arguing that Poppy shouldn't be separated from her siblings, that she doesn't even know them; her life is here, with us. Legally, Hannah was Poppy's guardian in the event that anything happened to Emma. That's what Emma had wanted in those early days when she was on her own with Poppy, in the days before us. Joe's solicitor had tried to assert that Poppy should be placed with someone neutral until all this had been sorted out properly, that since Hannah was living here with us it wasn't really a good solution for the care of Poppy to be given to Hannah. Luckily, the social workers had disagreed. You cannot remove a child from her life on a whim; you cannot expect her to adjust to living apart from the life she had always known. Poppy was allowed to stay with us, in the only home she had ever known.

I'd tried to talk to Poppy about it, but she'd been confused. Her little, sad eyes had looked at me in wonder.

"I don't want to see another Daddy; I don't need another one. I've got you," she had said to me, softly.

"I know, but the lady who came to our house said that it would be good if you could try. You'll be in a big playroom and there will be lots of toys?"

"I've got toys here."

"Poppy, sometimes we have to do things that we don't want and we don't like to do. When you're a bigger girl, you'll understand why. If you don't like going, if you don't want to talk, that's fine. Make sure you tell the nice lady why."

"Why can't Finn come?" she asked me, pleadingly.

"You're special, Poppy, because you have two Daddies who love you. Most people only have one. Finn can't go with you because Joe isn't Finn's Daddy. But maybe we can see if he can come with you, one time?" I tried to bargain with her, thinking that even suggesting it to the social worker was going to be more of a hassle than it was really worth.

Our case worker had given us a good children's book about the difference between a Dad who lives with you, and a Dad you never see. It was a clever little book, really, trying to explain in the simplest terms how a child can end up with two fathers. I was worried that Poppy wouldn't understand it, but I needn't have been. She certainly understood the how and why, but what she didn't understand was why she was being made to do something that she didn't want to do. In Poppy's world, she had one father, and, frustratingly, that's how she wanted things to stay.

Social Services didn't like the fact that Poppy had grown up with a very limited version of the truth, but, in all honesty what could we have done? Poppy began calling me Dad because she wanted to, not because we made her. There was a void in her life, something missing that other children had. She had no memories of her real father because, quite simply, he had walked out and never looked back. How can you tell a child that they have another father, show them pictures, encourage emotions, and then, in another blow, state that the other father doesn't want to see them, doesn't want to know, or want to love them? Emma and I had talked about it and it had always seemed cruel. It had seemed to us that the right thing for Poppy, the least emotionally traumatic solution was just not to give him more than a passing thought, to let Poppy carry on living in her perfect little world until she was old enough to question it. The real truth could come later, when she was emotionally mature enough to deal with it.

Hannah had agreed to take Poppy to her first session in Kendal first thing tomorrow morning. It was unfortunate that the contact was scheduled to take place at the same time as my meeting with Jean Witton's husband. I tried to make myself feel better about it by reminding myself that I wasn't allowed in the room anyway. That I would only be able to watch Poppy from the other side, through a glass window in which I could see her, but she couldn't see me.

I was worried for Poppy, worried about how she was going to react to strangers. Worried that the report was going to reflect badly on us, that Poppy would appear withdrawn and sad, and it might seem that we were encouraging her to have negative thoughts towards Joe. Most of all, I felt guilty. Terrible, gut wrenching guilt that lay in the pit of my stomach every night. That my little girl was already having to deal with her mother lying in a hospital bed. That suddenly having to deal with this too – well, in my mind, it was too much. Too much for a girl of six-years-old to have to go through. I didn't want her to look back at this time with bitterness, because she quite simply couldn't even begin to understand.

Yet, my hands were tied. The court order had been made. Poppy would see her father twice a week. Failure of Poppy attending the sessions would reflect badly on us in court. My solicitor had told me that, with any luck, the contact sessions wouldn't go well. Joe had a long history of being unemotional towards others. Unless he could show genuine concern and empathy for Poppy, unless they could give her something that we couldn't, then, with any luck, the court would rule in our favour. The CAFCASS report would include information from all the people that Poppy knew, from all the people who had input into her life. From the people that knew she was happy and loved.

As I tucked Poppy into bed that evening, I could only hope that what we had would be enough. Our family was already torn at the seams. Losing Poppy would turn it to shreds. It would destroy us, and I really didn't know how we would cope if the court ruled in Joe and Rachel's favour.

Poppy was my daughter. I wouldn't let her go, not without a fight.

Chapter Twenty Six

Hannah

James left early for Morecambe on the day of the first of Poppy's contact sessions. Bob had come to look after Finn and Millie, and there was talk of taking them out for a wander down to the lake to feed the ducks. Poppy was due for her session at 10:00am, which meant that we had to be up and ready and out of the house for 9:15 to give us plenty of time to get to Kendal, get parked, and arrive at the centre.

Poppy was wearing leggings and a smock top with a grey cardigan with her brown, fluffy boots. She tended to choose clothes for comfort over fashion, and she wasn't the kind of girl to wear nice, pretty winter dresses with matching tights. The tights would be too itchy, she would complain, or the dress would flap around too much. She sat quietly in the car, as if contemplating her life, which was unusual. Poppy was usually a singer in the car - she knew all of the words to "One Direction" and would tap her feet eagerly to the music.

We parked the car and walked over to the centre. I understood that children went in the building one way, and the people having the contact another. The children were always allowed to leave first, and the people having contact had to remain in the building for an extra ten minutes or so. I supposed that such procedures were in place to safeguard the children - that not all people having contact would be upstanding pillars of the community. That there might be a real risk of children being followed on their departure. Or by desperate parents wanting to steal their children back.

I filled in all of the necessary paperwork. The woman who had come over to do the initial report on all of the children, June, would be Poppy's case worker. That meant she would interview all of the people that were involved in Poppy's life – her doctor, her teachers, her family, and close friends. She would conduct the parenting assessment on Joe and Rachel, but she would also do a more thorough report on James on how he could financially and emotionally, support Poppy. Her findings would eventually become one long report, which the family courts would then use to form the basis for their decisions on what would happen to Poppy.

June took Poppy through to the playroom, and I was left on the other side of the one-way mirror, in a room with a vending machine and a couple of tables. It reminded me of how swimming pool foyers used to be – plastic chairs and poor decorations. Instead of being able to look into a pool though, I saw into a treasure trove of children's activities. I watched as June took a chair that was placed at the edge of the room and started writing things down on her notepad, while Poppy ran to the table full of plastic animals. She would be allowed around five minutes by herself to get used to the room, before Joe and Rachel would enter from the other side.

I went over to the vending machine and ordered a tea, sat down, and waited.

It was interesting watching Joe and Rachel enter the room. It was immediately clear that they didn't really know what to do, or how to act. Joe towered over Poppy while she sat playing with the animals. Rachel bent down to her level and started talking to her. Poppy's face looked sad and angry. She didn't appear to answer whatever they were saying to her. A few moments later, Rachel gestured towards a painting table and Poppy nodded, her eyes looking towards the glass, knowing that I was watching on the other side. I couldn't take it. I couldn't be responsible for her sadness. I took my tea and went back to the reception area to find another woman, sitting, waiting.

"First time?" she asked me.

"Is it that obvious?" I asked, managing a weak smile.

"It gets easier, you know. The first time I came here, god, I was a bag of nerves. I still prefer not to watch the session through the glass. I find it all a bit strange and I would rather not be a part of it."

I nodded in agreement.

"How old is your child?" I asked her.

"I have two. They are two and four. Their father's been released from prison after a charge of GBH. Hopefully this is just a formality. I think he only wants to see the kids because he knows that it's a good way of getting to me, you know? But it's not going well for him either; our caseworker says that he doesn't seem to have much emotional attachment to the boys."

"How awful. Poppy's six. She hasn't seen her biological father in four years."

"Always the case, isn't it? It's always up to the mother to bring them up right."

"Oh, I'm not her mother. No, her mother, my best friend, is critically ill in Preston hospital. Apparently, that means he can swan in after all these years and claim her, that her stepfather doesn't have any rights."

The woman nodded. "Try not to worry, love; it'll come right. Family courts are much better than they used to be, and they don't like altering the arrangements that were already in place for the child before."

"I hope you're right, because I'm not sure how Poppy would cope with such an upheaval to her life right now," I managed.

I looked up at the clock. There was still an hour to go.

*

By the time Poppy had finished, I'd checked my emails twice, read a few chapters of my book, caught up on texting various people the most up-to-date news about Emma, and drunk no less than three cups of tea. Poppy came out smiling, which was a good thing. June said the session had gone as expected - that Poppy had been reluctant to engage with Joe, but had been more willing to talk to Rachel. She said that Poppy might improve with time.

As we left the building, I held back from asking Poppy too many questions, held back from prying. Instead, I suggested that we went for a girl's lunch in McDonalds, so long as she didn't tell Finn. Poppy's eyes sparkled as she sat down at a table while I went to order. She was munching away on her nuggets when she said it:

"I don't like my new Daddy. He told me I could have my own bedroom in London, and I could have pony lessons if I wanted."

I held back. Joe had been told he wasn't allowed to put any such ideas into Poppy's head. That he wasn't allowed to try and bribe her into a new life with false promises. I made a mental note to call June when we got home.

"If the judge decides that I have to go to London, do I really have to go? Even if I don't want to? They won't make me, will they?"

For the first time in her short life, I looked up at her, preparing myself to lie. I couldn't tell her the truth. I couldn't tell her that if that were what was decided in court then there would be nothing we could do about it. That Joe and his wife could do whatever they wanted. Surely, it wouldn't come to that? Surely, it couldn't.

"If that's what the judge decides, sweetie, then there's other things we can do. And if the judge says that you're going to London for now, then you can be sure that I'll be with you. I'll find somewhere to live nearby, so that you won't be all on your own. So that you can spend your time with me too. Because that's what Mummy wants - for you to be happy."

I immediately felt guilty for lying to her. For pretending that all of this was just something that could be easily fixed. For pretending that her opinions mattered. For pretending that I could shelter her from the worst of it, if that's what it really came down to. I watched her as she finished her lunch, wondering, silently, what would really happen if the courts sided with Joe. I wouldn't let them take her. I wouldn't let Emma's wishes be cast aside. We needed to get some kind of dirt on Joe, something that would make him look questionable in court. For the first time in days, I thought of Jim and his dodgy contacts. I pulled my mobile out of my pocket and began to dial.

Chapter Twenty Seven

Edd

Steven Brann took his time coming to answer the front door, but as he opened it to us, I could see that he recognised Mary but couldn't quite place her. Understandably, really, given that it had been thirty years since he had organised the adoption of Emma and Sophie.

"Edd Harper," I said, extending my hand. He took it and shook gently, albeit a little confusingly.

"I'm a private investigator. This is Mary Evans. You might remember her? In the early 1980s, you organised the adoption of her and Bob's two daughters - Emma and Sophie Steel. We have some questions to ask you - may we come in?"

It was more of an order than a request. Steven looked around anxiously before stepping aside and letting us in. We followed him into the kitchen, where he gestured for us to sit at a table and flipped the switch on a kettle. He probably hadn't realised that his hands were twitching, fiddling. He was worried about where this might go.

"Nice house you have here. Bought it for a bit of a bargain, didn't you?" I asked him. It was a stab in the dark, but it didn't take a genius to realise that it hadn't been long after the girls' adoption that Mr. Brann suddenly had enough money to buy a house. He squirmed uncomfortably in his seat.

Before he had a chance to answer the question, Mary added,

"My daughter, Emma, was in an accident. She has three little children of her own now," Mary said, passing Steven a photo of Poppy, Finn and Millie across the table.

"Emma is in a bad way," I told Steven. "It's unlikely that she's going to recover. In fact, it's more a case now of how long it's going to take her to deteriorate. The police aren't interested in finding the driver of the vehicle that knocked her down. But her husband and her parents, understandably, want answers. Emma was a young woman in the prime of her life. She had close family, good friends. There isn't anyone we can think of that might want to cause her harm.

"Emma was plagued with nightmares as a child. Now, I strongly believe that they have something to do with her past. Sophie tried to trace their biological parents when she was eighteen, but she didn't get very far. Records that should have been kept had disappeared. There was no information, anywhere, on where they had come from, or what had happened to them before they were adopted by Mary and Bob. We've come here today to see if we can jog your memory. To see if you can remember anything about how they came to be in the care home. To find out if anything happened in Emma's past that could have instigated this accident, and if so, we want justice to be sought. Those three little children are going to grow up without their mother. There are things about the adoption that don't make sense, you see. Perhaps you can explain them?"

Steven Brann nodded. I could see that, at heart, he was a good family man.

"I'll make us a pot of tea. This might take some time," he replied.

As Steven started messing around with cups, teapots, milk jugs, and a plate of biscuits, I glanced around the kitchen. There were photos of his two teenage boys on holiday in Florida, and photos of him and his wife in some seemingly exotic places. I seriously doubted that his wife's flower shop managed to pay for such luxury holidays.

Mary took charge of pouring the tea and handing round the biscuits. I took a large gulp of mine, eyeing both Mary and Steven.

"You do remember the girls, Steven?" Mary asked him. I sensed his body relax a little before he answered the question.

"Of course. They were such beautiful girls. Hard to believe..." he began, but then suddenly realised that he was starting at the end of his story instead of the beginning.

"Anything I tell you, I assume, will be off the record?" he asked me.

"I can't guarantee anything, but if it is possible to keep your name out of it then yes, you have my word that I'll try not to tarnish your name," I said.

Steven nodded.

A longer than necessary silence filled the room, as if Steven couldn't really decide on where exactly to begin.

"Perhaps you can start by telling us when you began working in the home?" Mary asked him. I smiled. Mary would make a good side-kick.

"I started working as a social worker. Then, after a few years, I got a job for the local authority in Chester, on the panel that organises adoptions and fostering in and around the area. At the same time, I was working as the assistant manager of the care home, which was also run by the Local Authority. Working as both allowed me to work closely with the children - to understand what each child needed in the run-up to adoption or fostering. I worked hard to get the children the help and support that they needed in the home, to try to get them back on the right path, but it was difficult. We didn't receive much funding. We had to count every coloured pencil, every sheet of paper. Children shouldn't have to live like that...

"After a few years, the old manager moved on – he was offered a job working for the Local Authority in Manchester, the same job but more children, so a higher pay-scale. I was then offered his job and I took it. In the short term, I could work both jobs. It was likely that I wasn't going to be the manager of the care home for long, because the future of the home was becoming uncertain. They wanted more children to be in foster placements, which the government felt was more similar to the lives they would live afterwards - even those children who were placed in the home as a short-term, temporary measure. For example, if a single parent with no family suddenly found herself in hospital, then it would fall on the local authority to take care of the children. They wanted the children to be integrated in society, rather than segregated as they were - locked away and out of sight. The council started to increase the financial incentives for people to take on foster children, gave them bigger council houses. Just before Emma and Sophie came to us, we were running with around half the amount of children that we had previously been caring for.

"This was difficult. Mandy and I, we'd been married for a few years. Her Mum was ill, so Mandy had to pack in her job as a teacher. The hours were too long and she couldn't manage it all; she was an only child, so there was no one else you see - she had to be there for her. We lived in a tiny house but money was tight. I was working overtime to pay the mortgage.

"There were nearly twenty children in the care home at the time. I'd been working hard to get more prospective parents through the system – and because my other job was on the panel, it didn't take too much extra work to make that happen. Funding cuts were hitting us hard. They didn't want to pay the extra amount of money it cost to run the children's home and we needed to find the children permanent homes before the care home was shut down completely. It was only a matter of time.

"I was working on the morning that they brought the girls in. We'd had a call from the police to say that they had been recovered from an incident in London and it wasn't safe for them to be kept in that area so they were being transferred here, to Chester. It happens from time to time. It's not as uncommon as you might think – especially when there is domestic violence. People like to use children against their partners, try to get them back, or cause them harm. It's like the children are a pawn in a game of chess. They don't care about the children, really. It's better that they are moved on, placed with people who can give them a better life – a good life. I was the one who completed all of the paperwork in the office while the girls were taken for a medical – we checked their weight, height, eyes, general reflexes, etc. It's all changed since then, of course, integrated services. If a child doesn't have a red child health book with them, or if the vaccinations aren't stamped, that's an immediate red flag.

"So, I was filling all the paperwork out, there were some sections for me and there were some sections for whoever brought the children in to complete. It's so that all the information is there - for later, when they come to be adopted. There's a box on the form about things that a child may have seen that could have caused them stress, or harm. That's when the officer looked up at me. I could see that there was a clear hesitation. That there was something that he didn't want to write on the form...."

I glanced across at Mary while Steven Brann paused. She was poised, like me, like a cat ready to pounce on a mouse. We were hanging onto his every word.

"What...what did he write?" Mary asked him.

"He didn't write anything. He looked up at me – and said, *'If I write what happened on this form, no one will want those girls.'* I looked at the picture he had brought with him. Such lovely, happy-looking children. So beautiful. I said to him, *'Between you and me? I'll be in charge of the adoption; I'll make sure that they get a good home. But it's important for us to know where they came from. It's important so that we can help them move on'*. I could see that he was uncomfortable, that there were things he didn't want to admit to me. I was used to uncomfortable situations - child abuse was a day-to-day reality for me. But I'll never forget the words he said to me that day – as he looked me straight in the eye *'These children have witnessed a murder.'* Then, quick as the wind, he signed the bottom of the form, and left.

Chapter Twenty Eight

__Mary__

A silence filled the room. I looked across at Edd, who didn't seem as shocked by the revelation as myself. How could this be? Surely, this couldn't be right? If the children had witnessed a murder then surely their faces would have been all over the tabloids? Surely, the authorities would have told us something; they wouldn't have kept that crucial information from us? Unless, maybe, they were worried about keeping the girls safe. Maybe they were worried that the killer would come looking for them and would strike again?

"What do you mean?" I managed to ask Steven.

"I'm afraid that I wasn't told all of the specifics," he began, "But I did worry about how what they might have seen may have affected them negatively. After the policeman left, I went down to see the children. Emma was four, and Sophie one. Sophie could walk, and would follow Emma around like a shadow. We liked to keep the children who were under two years old separate at night time, because they used to wake up more often; their sleep patterns were more disturbed. But Emma wouldn't be separated from her sister; it was as if she thought that she could keep Sophie safe. In the end, we had to move them into a small bedroom together; it was the only way they would sleep at night – cuddled up in the same bed. It made me wonder about the kind of life they'd had before..."

"So, you knew that the children had witnessed a murder? Why did that make you hurry along the adoption proceedings? Why were they placed with a family quicker than the other children?" Edd asked him.

"The girls were settling into the home well. Though they weren't too keen on mixing with the other children very much. I had started filling out the assessment forms that were needed for placing them with adoptive parents. At the time, we had a few sets of parents going through the paperwork to be approved to adopt. Then, one day in my office, I received a strange call.

"The call was from a man, claiming to be the girls' father; he wanted to meet with me to discuss what the girls had seen and to talk to me about how to keep them safe. Sometimes people working for the adoption panel have been known to take payments for hurrying along certain adoptions. The man said that he would make it 'worth my while'. Of course, it's a sack-able offence and I could have lost my job over it. Looking back, I shouldn't have manipulated the system as I did. But what would you have done? We really needed the money. The girls needed to be kept safe. In my mind, it was a win-win situation.

"So I met the man at Chester Zoo one afternoon, near the lions. He told me that their mother and brother had been shot by an intruder while the girls were in the house – a bad burglary gone wrong. The police recovered the children from inside a wardrobe where they had been hiding – the mother and brother lay dead in the room next door. The man said that he couldn't take the girls, because it wasn't safe - the killer was out there and they might want to use the children as collateral, to get money. He was insistent that they must be taken in and moved somewhere safe, that they weren't safe. He offered me £500,000 cash, up-front. A following £20,000 every year that the girls were kept safe until they were eighteen."

"You placed the girls with us because we were moving away?" I asked Steven.

"He placed the girls with you because he thought that you were the best people to keep them safe and give them a good life," Edd interjected, "The person who paid him didn't want a quick-fix solution. He wanted to make sure the girls would be safe in the long term."

Steven nodded. "There were a lot of people we had who were going through the paperwork that would allow them to adopt. Even then, it was a longer process than most people think. I went through all of the files with a fine toothcomb, of every set of parents we had going through the system. Mary and Bob were planning to move north, which was a big plus. They were older and more financially stable. I spoke to the lady who was going through all of their paperwork; she'd been into their house and interviewed them. I discussed with her the possibility of them having the two girls; I told her that I thought they would be perfect for them and I was keen for the girls to stay together. It was much harder to place siblings, you see. I knew that the girls would have a good life with the Evans'."

"So you hurried along the paperwork, had Mary and Bob approved, then what?" Edd asked.

"I met the man only once more, to give him the address of the house that Mary and Bob had moved to with Emma and Sophie. We used the money to put down a deposit on this place, and we moved in. I was given the number of a safety deposit box and a key. Every year to the day, without fail, the £20,000 was in there."

"You never saw him again, this man?" I asked him. It was as if we were all waiting with baited breath for Steven to reveal the man's true identity.

"He never told me his name and I never had a phone number for him. He told me that I would find him by the lions on the exact day and time of our first meeting, every year from that day. But I've never had any reason to contact him. I saw his picture, though, in a major tabloid two summers after the girls had been adopted. His wife had given birth to a son."

"Steven, who was he?" I asked, softly.

"His name is Andrew Cook."

I gasped. Even Edd looked shocked. Andrew Cook was a man from a very affluent family. His parents owned an oil company. They were worth billions of pounds. Surely, someone with that much money at their fingertips could afford to keep their daughters safe? The royal family seem to manage it, after all.

I could see Edd was trying to work something else out, while he was scribbling on his notepad.

"The day that you first met Andrew Cook, the day that he promised to be at the lions at the same time for each year afterwards. That must be roundabout now?" he asked Steven.

Steven nodded.

"It's tomorrow, at 2p.m"

Chapter Twenty Nine

James

I pulled up outside the restaurant where I had arranged to meet Jean Witton's husband, Roy. It was one of those British-American diners, but the car park was relatively quiet. Inside, I walked over to a booth and ordered a coffee.

Roy Witton wasn't how I expected him to be. He was tall, but thin and wiry. He looked anxious - as he took his seat opposite me and ordered a cappuccino.

"Thanks for meeting me and I am so sorry to hear about your wife," I said. Roy nodded.

"How is Emma?" he asked.

"She's not doing well. I'm heading there after this. Her organs are starting to fail. The doctors don't think she's going to make it." It was the first time that I had managed to reveal this information to anyone other than our immediate family. The first time that I hadn't let the realisation of Emma's deterioration make me feel angry and bitter.

"At least, with Jean, it was quick. She wasn't lingering; she wasn't in pain."

I wondered for a moment if it would have been better that way; if Emma had been found dead that morning. I decided it wouldn't have been any less devastating. Yet, there would have been an end to it all. There wouldn't have been all this false hope - all the expectation for her to get better.

"I didn't know that Emma had been in touch with Jean. In fact, I didn't even know who Jean was. Emma had left a note." I explained to Roy about the folder, about how I had learned that Jean had been killed.

"I told Jean that she should have told Emma about Iris all those years ago. But after Iris was gone, Jean had said that it wasn't fair on Emma, that she couldn't change what had happened; it wouldn't bring Iris back. She got in contact with Emma again once, when she was pregnant with the oldest child – Polly?"

"Poppy."

"Sorry, Poppy. Anyway, it didn't seem right to her to go stirring up all that emotion when Emma was pregnant again. So more years went by. Then she made contact with her again. Jean had been through a tough time with breast cancer, but she'd made it in the end. She had said that she needed to tell Emma the truth, in case anything ever happened to her, that she couldn't die with secrets. So she told her."

"Told her what, exactly?" I asked him.

"When Iris was taken from her that day, she wasn't dead. They hooked her up again to a load of monitors in another room."

"But why would they do that?" I said to Roy, wondering aloud.

"I don't really know. But it took another few days for them to lose her properly. I believe they used her body for medical science."

"But Iris was buried, a few days after she died. Are you saying that she was still alive then? Still in Manchester hospital?"

"It's likely, yes."

"But why?" I asked Roy. He shrugged his shoulders.

"I don't suppose that many babies are donated for medical science?" he said, wondering.

"I'll be honest with you, James. It seems highly suspicious that as soon as Jean had told Emma what she believed to be the truth, she was knocked down. It's almost as if someone wanted to keep the truth hidden. Someone out there wanted to keep whatever happened under wraps."

I nodded in agreement. Why would anyone do that to a young mother? Tell them that their baby had died when she carried on living? Prevent a proper burial? I wondered what had happened to the tiny body of Iris. I wondered what actually lay beneath her grave. This was a matter for the police. They were going to have to excavate.

Roy handed me a piece of paper. It had a phone number and an address written neatly across it.

"That's the private number and home address for the medical director of the hospital at the time. He lives in Lancaster now. Shall we go and pay him a visit?" Roy asked.

"Let's go," I replied.

Chapter Thirty

James

Roy Witton had done his research. He had figures for the number of babies that had been born and never left Manchester Children's Hospital in the year that Emma had lost Iris. He had lists of all the nurses and doctors who were working on the ward at the time that Jean and Emma had been there with their babies. Two of the doctors had left soon after, under suspicious circumstances, and a trainee doctor, who was doing a ward rotation, soon left for another hospital. Roy suspected major foul play and negligence of care to the tiny infants. He remembered how distraught Jean had been to find the doctors standing around a barely-alive Iris, as if she were a battery hen and could be treated with such disregard, as if her life didn't matter. If Jean's thoughts were true, there were some serious questions to be asked.

I called the local police and told them that Iris's grave needed to be excavated, to make sure that she was, in fact, in there and that there were now some serious questions surrounding her death and the duty of care that the hospital had to these vulnerable children. I then followed Roy's car to Lancaster.

As he pulled down a quiet lane and parked his car, I quickly pulled out my mobile and text

Hannah to see how Poppy had managed at her first contact session. I wasn't expecting to get home until later, after I'd been to see Emma, and I didn't think I could wait that long to find out how it had gone with Joe and Poppy. I made a mental note to call Poppy's caseworker later on, to see if she could shed any more light on things.

The house we were looking up at was large. Slowly and carefully, we walked up to the front door. Roy knocked loudly. We waited.

No answer.

"Let's have a wander around?" Roy suggested. We wandered around the house, which was no mean feat in itself. We looked through the windows, trying to get an idea on what kind of person lived inside. A large pile of letters lay inside the front door. The house looked like it had been empty for days.

"What do we do now?" I asked him.

"We've phoned the police. We can tell them we paid a visit and that he wasn't in. But I suppose there is nothing else that we can do until the excavation has taken place. If Iris isn't in there, then who is? Can he ascertain his movements on that evening that Jean was knocked down? What about Emma?"

Roy was right. There were too many things that didn't add up. I suspected that maybe they had used Iris's body to their own gain. That Jean had uncovered the tip of an iceberg, and she was taken out before something was uncovered.

I took the list of nurses who were working on the ward at the time of Iris's death. One by one, I would call them. I would find out what was going on. I would find out, not just for Emma, but for Jean.

    Somewhere, someone had answers, and I wasn't going to rest until I found them.

Chapter Thirty One

<u>Mary</u>

We drove the car back to the hotel without much conversation. There was so much to take in and absorb, so many things that I had just learnt about my daughters.

I knew that I had to call Bob straight away from the hotel and tell him the latest news. He had been right all along to think that the girls' mother had been dead, but I wondered about the father. Is it a selfless act to send your daughters away to safety, or was it more selfish, and if so, just what was he trying to hide?

I also realised that I should phone Sophie and tell her to keep her wits about her while we carried on trying to work out the details about the adoption - not to go wandering around alone at night, to make sure that people knew where she was. But was there really any need to worry her? To put that kind of uncertainty in her mind? She had been kept safe and well for all these years without any problems. There had been no murderers knocking on our door looking for them, no strange incidents.

I found it hard to believe that someone who went to great length, financially, to keep the girls safe, could be the one responsible for Emma's accident. I googled Andrew Cook and could find no mention of his two adopted daughters - of Emma and Sophie. There was only mention of a son, Henry, with the woman he had married after the girls had come to live with us.

Edd had found the details of a murder in London, which remained largely unreported, given the brutality of the crime. The police had walked into a bloodbath, and the killer was never found. There was a reference to the dead woman leaving behind two daughters, but no reference of them being in the house at the time of the crime. No reference to the police pulling them from the wardrobe, of driving the frightened children miles away, and dropping them off at the care home in Chester. Why hadn't Andrew Cook intervened? Why hadn't he taken the girls in? What kind of father was he?

Over dinner, in the hotel that evening, we talked about tomorrow's meeting with Andrew. Edd said that we had to remain calm, that we couldn't start shouting accusations. That we would have to appeal to his better nature. We needed to know more about the girl's mother, about why she had been killed. We needed to know who he thought the killer was and if they were still a danger to the girls, all these years later.

I felt that we were making good progress, even if it was all a bit much for me emotionally, to take in. I felt bad that all of this had been in the background of the girls' lives and we had never known. Sophie's fear of small spaces suddenly became quite rational. Who knew how many hours the girls had been shut inside that wardrobe before the police had found them? Emma and her nightmares – obviously she had been old enough to remember some of the horrors of that day but had been too young to rationalise the thoughts that went behind them, to make sense of what she had seen on that awful day.

I hoped that the girls would be able to get through this, emotionally, that was if Emma ever really recovered from what had been done to her. But most of all, I hoped that Andrew Cook had some good answers for letting go of his girls, because it didn't matter to me how much money he has or how many homes he had in foreign countries. He had let go of his family and he had never come back to claim them. He had lived a life in which the girls had no place and been no more than a passing thought. If he had really wanted to keep his daughters safe, then they would have been better off with him - in a house with bulletproof windows, with Rottweiler's guarding the doors. There were still many things about the actions of Andrew Cook that just didn't make sense.

Chapter Thirty Two

Edd

Mary and I spent the morning pretending that everything was normal. That the world in which we lived was a safe place. That we hadn't just learned about the events that had happened in Emma and Sophie's past. We ate a late breakfast in the hotel, and Mary went for a wander around some nearby shops while I called Sarah to let her know how we were getting on with the investigation.

By eleven o'clock, I'd had enough of hanging around the hotel waiting. I suggested to Mary that we head over to the zoo, buy our entrance tickets and have some lunch in the café and just wander around and admire the animals, which would at least be a change of scenery for us, so we did just that.

For December, the zoo was quieter than I thought it would have been. We wandered around and then sat watching the chimpanzees playing with some empty plastic bottles for some time. Mary told me that she and Bob had brought the girls here once, in the early days, when they had contact with the children but they weren't legally theirs yet. I'd never been a big zoo fan, and hadn't been to Chester zoo before, but I was amazed at the quantity of animals that the zoo held and the quality of their living environments. We had been to Flamingo Land once or twice when I was a little lad, and my memory was of beautiful, majestic animals locked inside small cages with nothing to do, and sad, haunting expressions. I was glad that things had changed, that the care of the animals came before the needs of the humans who came to see them.

I had googled a picture of Andrew Cook before we had set off that morning, so I knew who I was looking out for. I must admit, it was a little daunting. Andrew Cook was a man with both money and power. He was probably used to getting his own way – he wouldn't be used to making compromises and answering questions that he didn't want to answer.

Twenty minutes before two o'clock, we made our way over towards the lion enclosure. The irony of the moment wasn't lost on me, since it certainly felt like I was about to walk right into a lion's den. Mary and I stood together; to the outside world we were just a normal, middle-aged couple watching the lions, who didn't seem at all interested in what was going on around them. Eventually, at just after two o'clock, Andrew Cook appeared beside us.

Andrew Cook was tall and well-built, his greying hair was cut short, and even though he was wearing casual clothing, he wasn't someone you would want to mess with, or double cross.

"Mr. Cook," I acknowledged him. He continued to look forward at the lions instead of making eye contact with me.

"I'm Edd Harper and this is Mary Evans, Emma's mother. We need to talk with you urgently about some recent developments...if that's okay?"

Mr. Cook didn't respond immediately.

"I heard about the accident," he finally said. "Is she ok?" He looked across at Mary. I was glad that I'd had the sense to bring her along. Mary had pricked at his conscience. Perhaps Andrew wasn't such a heartless soul after all.

"She's stable, for now but it isn't looking good," Mary responded.

"I've got a suite at the Chester Grosvenor; I book the same one every year. Would you mind relocating there? I sense that we are going to need some privacy. There's a car out front"

It was more of an order than a request, but I didn't flinch. There was nothing worrying about it. In fact, it made more sense than talking about sensitive issues in front of a pride of lions. I nodded to Mary.

"Of course, lead the way," I replied. We followed Andrew to the car, and didn't speak another word until we were all sat round the table in the Presidential Suite.

*

Mary spent a good twenty minutes filling Andrew in on Emma. She started with the time that she and Bob had moved north, filling him in on all the important milestones that he had missed along the way – ballet medals, GCSEs, university. She also told him, straight out, that she was a Jehovah's Witness. Interestingly, he didn't bite at the new information. He didn't even frown. As she was telling him about Emma's time as a nurse and her move back up north when she was pregnant with Poppy, someone came and brought tea and cakes.

Between us, we filled him in on the week before Emma's accident. We told him about James and their other two children, and the house that they lived in just outside of Ambleside. Mary explained how Bob and I had been friends as children and how she had enlisted my help to track down Emma and Sophie's biological parents.

"I admit that I have remained in the shadows for all of the girls' lives. It's something I regret, but it's something that I did for their own safety. We'll get to that later. So you went looking for Mr. Brann? And what exactly did he tell you?" Andrew asked.

"He told us how the girls had arrived in the care home, about his one-time meeting with you, and about the financial arrangement that you made regarding finding the girls a good and suitable home," I told him.

"It's partly one of the reasons I went to Brann. He was a good man and he did right by the girls. But I knew that if anyone came looking for information about the girls' parents, he would point them in my direction. It's one of the reasons that I made the arrangement about the lions. I wanted to be contactable in the case of an emergency.... But, of course, no one could have predicted this."

"I wonder," Mary began, looking at Andrew, "if you could tell us the truth? From the beginning? About how the girls' mother died in such a horrific situation, and why? It goes without saying that I am worried that whoever took the girls biological mothers life may be hell-bent on revenge. That they might be the one who is responsible for what has happened to Emma."

Andrew met my gaze before answering Mary.

"Firstly, I hope you're not in a rush, because I believe this is going to take some time?"

"Not at all," I told him.

"Good," he replied. "Then there are two things that I believe you should both know, before I begin. The most important being that the person responsible for the girls' mother, Elizabeth's, death could not possibly be the person responsible for Emma's accident. The man who took Elizabeth's life in such cold blood was caught and killed. The other thing is that, although I love both Emma and Sophie dearly, and I have indeed kept a watchful eye on them over the years, the truth of the matter is – I'm not their father."

Chapter Thirty Three

Hannah

Back in Emma and James home after the contact session, life went on as normal. James was out, but the children ran around and played as if they didn't have a care in the world. After speaking with Jim, I felt a little more at ease with the situation. He's going to call in some favours and see if he can find anything out about Joe and his new wife. I know it seems a little callous, but I can't let them take Poppy. It would ruin James. It would destroy the happy little girl that she was.

I planned to head over to the hospital again tomorrow to see Emma. I found it very difficult, sitting by her bedside. Her spirit was gone. I could talk at her, but her essence was all but dried up. I couldn't help but feeling that this wasn't how she would have wanted to be living her life. That she wouldn't have wanted James sitting with her for all those hours, when he should have been enjoying life with their children.

When James arrived back from his meeting with Roy Witton, he filled me in on the day's events. I could hardly believe it. What exactly had the hospital done to poor little Iris? I remembered the look on Emma's face in the months after her first daughter's death – the pain and the sadness. Who would do that? Who could be so cruel?

James said that the excavation and subsequent post-mortem of Iris's body would occur in the next twenty-four hours. They would have a better idea then of what they were dealing with and of what the hospital had done wrong. I wondered how they could have done something so terrible. There were laws to protect children in our country, especially children who were vulnerable. You couldn't just let them down like that, could you?

After the children had gone to bed, we opened a bottle of wine. We edged closer and closer to each other as the wine started to disappear. James went to get another bottle. I was enjoying the company. For a moment, I forgot all about my problems with Jim. I forgot about Emma lying in that hospital bed alone.

Was it a surprise then that I didn't resist as James leant in to kiss me? Not really. Was it a surprise that I followed him upstairs without thinking twice?

In that moment, it didn't matter. In that moment, it felt right. Maybe, if I had known what would follow, I would have thought twice. Maybe, if my head wasn't all fuzzy from the red wine and if I hadn't had a long and stressful day.

I'm only human. I'm not going to make any excuses for my behaviour on that night, because, quite simply, there are none.

I followed James into the bedroom, and I closed the door behind us.

Chapter Thirty Four

James

When I awoke the next morning, my mind was temporarily confused. For a moment, I forgot all of the bad things that were going on in my life. For a moment, things were exactly as they should be. I had woken, as I so often do, next to my wife. The children were sleeping peacefully.

It was only when I stretched, grinned, and opened my eyes that I remembered: Emma was still lying in her hospital bed, and it was Hannah who was lying peacefully beside me.

I crept out of bed, put on my dressing gown, and walked downstairs. My stomach was filled with gut-wrenching guilt, churning over and over. How could I have done this to Emma? How could I have treated my wife with such disregard? The biggest problem of all – how on earth do Hannah and I move on from this? How do we carry on living together, sharing the children? I couldn't give Hannah what she really deserved. I couldn't be her knight in shining armour. I have a wife, a wife who needs me now more than ever.

It was early morning, still dark. I put the kettle on, tidied the living room, loaded clothes into the washing machine – I did anything to take my mind away from what I had done.

As dawn began to break, I went outside and let out the hens. The weather was warm for

December and there were a couple of eggs in the lay box. I wasn't as good as Emma was at sorting out the eggs and labelling the old from the new. It didn't take long until we were overrun with eggs, and who knew then which ones had been there a week or two, or which were fresh. I made a mental note to give some eggs to Emma's parents, and to be more rigorous in my labelling system.

While I was watching the hens with my coffee, Hannah came outside and stood beside me.

"James..." she began.

"Last night shouldn't have happened," I told her, sternly. I saw her face soften, her eyes questioning me. She was probably thinking that, although she knew it was wrong deep down, it felt right. I wanted to tell her that she was right, but my conscience just wouldn't allow it. I had been unfaithful to my wife. Once was a mistake. But twice? Nothing could be a mistake if it happened over and over again. I owed it to Emma to be faithful. I owed it to the children not to get involved with another woman when they already had so much else to contend with.

"This isn't going to ruin us, James, is it?" she asked me, cautiously.

"I hope not. You're a good friend, Hannah. But I can't do this. Not now...it isn't right and it can't go on."

Hannah nodded.

Inside the telephone began to ring.

"I'd better go and get that," I told her. "We're okay, aren't we? No hard feelings?" I asked her. She shook her head softly.

As I walked away from Hannah, back into the house, I didn't see the tears that had began to fall down her cheeks. Her soft, gentle sobs. I didn't tell her that everything would be okay, that we could work through this – although I knew that I should have. I felt worse than I'd ever felt before. I was letting down two women. The one who was lying, unconscious and unaware of the world, and the one who was standing right in front of me. But I had no idea how to make it all better for either of them.

Somehow, I managed to answer the phone before it went to answer phone, which was no mean feat in itself.

"Hello?"

"Mr Parker?" The voice asked.

"Yes?"

"I'm calling from the lab. We received the body from the exhumation of the grave and we worked on it overnight. We completed comprehensive DNA testing, and we can confirm that the body is that of Miss Iris Evans."

"Oh...thank you. That is good news," I managed to reply.

"We requested all the documentation from the hospital, and looked at the original autopsy report, and there is something a little strange...." he continued

"Please, go on," I urged.

"It seems that Iris didn't die from Edwards Syndrome, as was noted on her death certificate. Her cause of death was swelling to her brain that would be consistent with a head injury. Now, I'm no expert in paediatrics, but I imagine that the brain injury had come from her being dropped from a great height."

"Someone dropped her?" I asked him, dumbfounded.

"It would seem so. The medical records we have for visitors in and out of the hospital, state that Iris's father was the last person to see her alive. The doctors did all they could, but how could they have known? Clearly the incident wasn't logged."

"Hang on, are you telling me that Joe dropped her? That he didn't report the accident, or whatever it was, and that it caused her to decline?"

"That's right. At the time, they thought that it was the Edwards Syndrome. Children can deteriorate quite quickly. As I'm sure that you're aware, most of them don't even survive the birth. The hospital called the mother back as soon as they saw her stats dropping. Just after Iris died, they called a meeting, because such a rapid deterioration just didn't make sense. Because they had no proof of who exactly had done this, it was covered up, so to speak. It was likely that the hospital didn't want to be sued for medical negligence."

"How considerate of them," I managed.

"Well, I'll type up the report and send you a copy. It's up to you where you take things from here."

"Thank you," I said, as I hung up the telephone.

There was only one place in my mind that things could go from here. My life was bad enough. What happened to me wasn't what was in the forefront of my mind. I was thinking of Emma and Iris now, and of the danger that Poppy might be placed in if her father continued to persist in his right to custody.

I threw on some clothes, grabbed a banana, and went to Emma's old address book to find the address for Joe. There was only one person with the answers to what had happened to Iris. And I wasn't going to leave his house until I had them all.

*

I'd never been to Joe and Rachel's house. Why would I? It wasn't as if we were friends, or even had to try to be civil. He had cut all contact with Emma when he had decided he didn't want to be a part of Poppy's life. We never called him, never sent him copies of school reports, put school photos inside Christmas cards, or told him the dates of ballet shows. In my mind, either you're an active father, or you're not. Joe made his choices. He didn't deserve the luxury of the little details. Emma had his address written down in an old address book. It was there in case of a grave emergency. Both Emma and I liked to believe that if something really bad happened to Poppy, then he would show some kind of human compassion towards his daughter, his own flesh and blood. But after this revelation, I doubted it.

They lived on the outskirts of Manchester in a town called Bolton. It was a funny kind of place, all dark and dreary. Once a thriving town that dealt with textiles, it was now busy enough, but most of the factories had closed down. House prices were relatively reasonable compared to other places, yet it was still close enough to the M6 if you wanted to travel.

Joe and Rachel lived on the edge of the town, down a little lane. Their house belonged to a cull-de-sac of other detached houses. Their neighbours had an array of new and expensive cars on their driveways. There were no signs of any children living on this street; it was all too neat and orderly – no bikes littered the front lawns, no slides tucked away in the back gardens.

I parked the car outside and knocked on the door. Rachel answered.

"I'm here to see Joe, is he in?" I asked her.

She managed to keep the look of surprise hidden from her face as she surveyed me, as she wondered why I had come all this way to their house.

"He's just popped out for some bread, but he'll be back soon," she replied. She gestured into the house, and led me down a long corridor and into a large kitchen. Emma would have been mortified at this house. The walls were cream and unspoiled, the kitchen surfaces long and empty. Their rather expensive looking all-American fridge was not covered in drawings, or pictures of children. It all seemed a little clinical. It was almost as if the house were a show home, as if they didn't really live here at all.

"Would you like a coffee?" Rachel asked me, as I sat, waiting.

"No thanks, I doubt I'll be here for long," I replied. She shrugged her shoulders. I tried to have sympathy for the woman, after all, she wasn't responsible for someone else's actions even if she did have the stupidity to marry them – but it was hard because I knew that she was the main reason they had filed for custody of my daughter.

After around five minutes or so the front door went, and the sound of footsteps made their way into the kitchen.

"They had no seeded loaf, so I bought wholemeal," Joe said as he stepped into the kitchen. He looked me up and down before he acknowledged me.

"I thought you weren't interested in making negotiating?" he said to me, as if Poppy were one of his clients, as if her long-term welfare rested on an agreement which was cold and impersonal.

"I'm not," I told him, flatly. "I'm not here to talk about Poppy. I'm here to talk about Iris," I told him, meeting his gaze. His body suddenly became rigid, his senses heightened. His face resembled a white sheet – he looked like he had just seen a ghost.

"Shall we go into my office?" he asked me, after a moment of uncomfortable silence.

"You don't want your wife to hear what I have to say?" I asked him, threateningly. He avoided my gaze, which was enough confirmation that Rachel didn't have a clue about what was going on. I wondered if she even knew about Iris's existence.

"I think I'd like to listen, if it's all the same," Rachel said, softly. There was no response at all from Joe. He stood like a rabbit startled by headlights.

"Right, well, Emma had an interesting letter from a lady who had been in the hospital the same time that she had been there with Iris. Yesterday, I went to meet her husband. He told me that he believed that there had been some kind of cover-up at the hospital, that Iris's death hadn't been as Emma had thought. There was some information, which led up to the belief that Iris might have lived longer than we had thought, though we now know that isn't the case. They excavated her grave to confirm her identity, and had another thorough look at her autopsy report. Iris did die that day in the hospital, held by her mother. But the question isn't *when* anymore, is it Joe? The question is *how*?"

Rachel looked at me, confused. Joe didn't meet her eyes.

"Iris was the baby that Emma had first, before Poppy," he told her in an almost whisper.

"The coroner called me this morning. He told me that the last person to see Iris, before she started her rapid deterioration, was you, Joe. That the cause of Iris's death was, in fact, a trauma to her head. A trauma that is consistent with her being *dropped*. Yet, this is news to me and I'm sure that it'd be news to Emma if she were awake. Because you never told anyone that you dropped her, Joe, did you? And why is that? Because you were glad she was gone? Because you meant to do it? And you think, somehow, that after this revelation that you're going to get within an inch of *my daughter* again? You think that you're going to have Poppy to come and live with you? I hope you've got money to burn, and a bloody good lawyer. Because you mean nothing to Poppy, and that's exactly how it's going to stay."

Rachel's face looked suddenly green. "I think I'm going to be sick," she said, and fled from the room. Her husband didn't follow her, didn't try to comfort her. I wasn't surprised. I shook my head at him in disgust, and let myself out.

Chapter Thirty Five

Mary

You could have heard a pin drop in the presidential suite that afternoon. Edd and I were hanging onto every word of Andrew Cook. Looking at him now, I could see the lack of resemblance that he had to Emma and Sophie and yet...there were features of him that reminded me of them – a bit like you might say you had your grandfather's eyes, or your grandmother's complexion.

It made logical sense that he wasn't their father. It's easier to give away someone else's children, I imagined. It was easier to keep an eye on them from a distance, to make sure that they were safe, but not become too involved. After all, he had his own life to lead. But I still had a sense that we were missing a large portion of the story, and the most crucial part of it – how exactly had Andrew Cook become involved in this situation? Which piece of the jigsaw belonged to him?

As if sensing my thoughts, he began to speak again.

"Elizabeth was my sister. You probably wouldn't have found a great amount of information about her if you went looking." Andrew looked at Edd while he was saying this, waiting for the appropriate response.

"I found mention of a sister that had been...cast out, shall we say?" Edd replied.

"That's right. I was the eldest of the three of us. Elizabeth came next and then Robert. You're probably aware that our parents come from a privileged background? My grandfather, on my father's side, struck oil and it made us very wealthy. My father, naturally, worked in the company with him, travelling all over the world. We lived in a large house, just outside London. Our mother, god rest her soul, was patient and kind. We had a nanny, but my mother liked us to spend time with her every afternoon. She took us on walks around the gardens, liked to collect us from school when we were older. Our father didn't like it. He wanted her to be more professional. To him, the business came first and the children came second.

"Elizabeth was the golden child. She was pretty and bright, her hair was as white as snow, and her eyes glistened when you spoke to her. She was also daring and quite uncontrollable at times. She was, you see, spoiled. Mother showered her only daughter with gifts to make up for the times that she wasn't around. We boys were just left to get on with it, you see. Then, at boarding school, she got in with a bad crowd - a group of girls with very wealthy fathers. They dabbled in drugs, they stole from other pupils. In the end, Elizabeth was expelled, which meant she had to return home to a house where neither our mother or father could control her. In her early twenties, she took off with one of her school friends. They married in haste, and soon after, they had a son. Did she love him? Who really knows? She was cut off then, from the rest of the family.

"My father didn't like Elizabeth's husband's family, because he said that they treat the people who worked in their factories with disregard. My father may have been a well-off man, but he had high standards. He paid his workers far more than was necessary, even in countries where he could have gotten away with paying them less. He always understood that people had families to care for, children to feed. He also thought that if you paid your workers fairly, and treated them with respect, they, in turn, would be more loyal to the company – they wouldn't take days off when they were sick, wouldn't take any liberties. He was a good man.

"Anyway, so Elizabeth was now married. I kept in touch with her from time to time. Her husband, Ian, was not a kind man. Cutting her off from us meant that Elizabeth had very little money of her own. She relied on any money that Ian gave her. So when their son began school, Joshua, they called him, she began working. She was a good worker - she was bright, and efficient. She worked as a personal assistant for a private dentist. He treated her well. After some time, it became evident to me that they were having an affair. Ian remained a dominant and controlling man. I believe that Elizabeth felt trapped in a situation in which she had no control.

"Soon after, she became pregnant again. I had my suspicions about the baby's parentage, but I didn't question her, and nor did she offer any information to me. Joshua was five now. The next baby, a girl, was called Emily – though, obviously, you know her now as Emma. A few years later came another girl, Sophia, or Sophie, as you know her. Elizabeth was happy. She looked after the children. Ian was working away a lot and I think that it suited her. She started to look radiant, more like her former self. Then, one day, she asked me for money.

"She told me that she needed to get away from Ian, that it was time that she followed her heart. She was, of course, talking about setting up home with this dentist – the man who I thought was the father of the two little girls. I asked her outright and she didn't deny it. She told me that she felt suffocated. That she couldn't live her life like that anymore. I told her that it would take me a few days to be able to get hold of the kind of money she needed – enough to buy a house somewhere else, enough to disappear for a while with all the children.

"I didn't trust Ian. He was cool and calculating. I hired some people to watch him. That's when it all started to go wrong. One morning, a few days later, he paid a visit to Elizabeth's friend, the dentist. He shot him with a pistol, right through the heart. I sent word to Elizabeth, told her to leave the house immediately with the children - to pack up anything of great importance, but to just get right out of there. There was no doubt in my mind that he had found out about the affair, that Elizabeth was his next target.

"She told me that I was being overly dramatic, that Ian had left for work and wouldn't be back for hours. I told her that I was coming over, right away. I told her to humour me, to hide the children in case he turned up, to tell them that I was coming and they were playing a game of hide and seek. I could be at her house in less than thirty minutes. I told her to hurry.

"I could tell that Elizabeth didn't believe me. Of course, I hadn't told her what I knew about the dentist's death – I couldn't. I was not cruel or unkind. I couldn't tell her that the man she really loved, the man she planned to have a future with, was lying dead in a pool of his own blood. She had three children that she needed to take care of.

"So I set off, at speed, to Elizabeth's house. But when I arrived there, it was too late..."

Andrew let his voice trail off. His eyes filled with tears, as if he were re-living the awful day that his sister was killed. I knew what was coming, and I felt a lump in my own throat. This woman, Elizabeth, was, after all Emma and Sophie's biological mother. She was the one who had given them life. I owed her more than she could ever know. Edd handed me the box of tissues that was placed on the edge of the table. I smiled softly.

"When I arrived, it was immediately apparent that Ian had beaten me to it. The door was ajar. I followed a trail of blood to the living room, and there they were - Elizabeth and Joshua. They lay next to each other on the floor. Placed that way intentionally, for someone to find. They had both been shot, though Elizabeth seemed to have a wound only to her leg. It wasn't until later that we realised she had been strangled, that it was more than likely Joshua had stood in front of his mother to save her life. The bullet that should have gone through his mother's heart had shattered his brain. It was...just awful...

"I was frozen in that spot. I felt sick. I called Robert. He arrived less than five minutes later. We had to think quickly. Where was Ian? What had he done with the girls? Robert was angry, irrational. I knew that Ian owned an apartment on the other side of London. It was an apartment that Elizabeth had never known about. He'd been having affairs for years. Not just one woman either. Robert went after him. I gave him a gun. We didn't need to say the words to each other. We knew, there and then, that Robert would find him and kill him.

"I called the police. I went to the room next-door, because I just couldn't stay in there. I just couldn't see them like that. I wanted to cover them with a cloth, but I knew that I might tamper with the evidence. I wanted to close Elizabeth's eyes, to pretend that she was just sleeping.

"As I sat in the room next-door, for what felt like forever, I started to relax a little. When I was really still, I heard a soft noise coming from the wardrobe. The soft sound of breathing, of small little movements

"Without thinking about what I was really doing, I stood up. I opened the wardrobe. There they were, Emily and Sophia. Emily was holding Sophia on her lap, and they looked frightened. Frightened, but alive.

I grabbed them, clung to them, my tears soaked through Emily's grey cardigan. I took Emily by the hand, and I held Sophia on my waist.

'We heard a big bang,' Emily told me.

'It's ok, you're safe now. We're going to go to see your granddad. He's going to make sure your safe.' I told them.

"I took my two little nieces and I left the house. Luckily, I could shield them from the devastation in the room next door by taking them out of the back door. We drove straight to my father. Although he and Elizabeth had their differences in the past, I knew that he was the only one who could make this right. The only one who could guarantee that these children were not in danger.

"When we arrived the girls had relaxed a little in my presence. I handed them over to my mother. She made a fuss over them, gave them ice-cream. She sent her cleaner out to the shops to buy them new clothes and toys.

"I found my father in his study, with Robert. As I closed the door behind me, I looked up at them.

'He's gone,' Robert said to me. A silence filled the room.

'The police have taken the bodies to conduct a full autopsy. They have cordoned off the room to search for DNA,' my father added.

'What do we do now?' I asked.

'We keep the girls here. I'll make enquiries. Just because Ian is gone, doesn't mean that they are safe now. It doesn't mean that nobody else will come looking for them' my father added.

'We are a family. We will do what normal families do. We will protect our own and we will pray to Jehovah. He will keep those girls safe - I am sure of it.'

"So that is exactly what we did."

I looked up at Andrew, clutching my tear-soaked tissue. It should have surprised me that Jehovah had a hand in us receiving the girls, but it didn't. We are like one extended family - we look after each other in our hour of need. I realised then that it hadn't been a coincidence that the girls had ended up in a care home in Chester. That we were the best parents for them, not only because of our ability to love but because of our faith. From one Witness to another, we were the best parents because we believed.

Chapter Thirty Six

<u>Edd</u>

We didn't leave Andrew Cook until late that evening. We had learned so much from him about the girl's biological parents, about their mysterious past. It was a shame that his parents had both passed away, though he assured us that he and his wife kept an eye on the girls, that they knew they were safe and loved by Mary and Bob.

I know that Mary had softened to Andrew. She had begun to see him as a real person with human compassion. She told him, as we were leaving, that she hoped he would come and meet Sophie, as an adult, and Emma's children. I knew from my own experience of losing touch with family, that Andrew was sincere when he said that he would. He had always looked on at the girls from a distance, the nieces that had grown up without knowing their uncle. That time was gone, but there was plenty of time left for them to make that up and become reacquainted. I wondered, to myself, if Emma would have any recollection of Andrew - if she had been well enough today. Or, whether her mind had simply blocked out all of the events from that terrible day. Perhaps we would never know.

We stopped in Preston, on the way back, to see how Emma was progressing. She was just as we had left her. Stable, with no improvement either way. It was a frustrating time for Mary and Bob, a time that was really testing their faith in the one true, Jehovah God.

As we drove back up the M6 towards Kendal, I felt a weight lift off my shoulders. We had achieved more than I thought was possible in our visit to Chester. We had put together a very large part of Emma and Sophie's childhood. Yet, still, we didn't have the answers. We were no closer to understanding who had done this to Emma.

I wondered, silently to myself, if the police had been right. If she had been knocked down by a drunk driver who simply didn't have enough of a conscience to own up to their crimes. A very odd and, yet, very real event, which was entirely unplanned and random. But, still, I had a niggling of doubt. This wasn't a big city where people lived anonymous lives. This was Ambleside. The place where everyone knew everyone. The place where people went out to get shopping, leaving the front door unlocked, without a passing thought of being burgled, of coming home to find the flat-screen HD TV exactly as they had left it. People looked out for each other here. Surely, someone knew something?

I knew that I was going to have to be a lot more systematic now in my approach to finding out who had done this. I was going to have to search through every single haystack before I found the needle. But I would find it. I do not admit to failure. I do not give up on cases, especially ones that are so close to home. I was a believer of many things, but I always believed in the power of good over evil. I knew that with all the positive energy coming from all the people who had known and loved Emma, we would win in the end. I wouldn't give up until that happened.

Chapter Thirty Seven

Sophie

To say that I was shocked about what my Mum and Edd had found out in Chester, would be the biggest understatement I had made in my entire life. And yet, once I knew the truth, many things made sense.

Emma had remembered our mother, I was sure of it. I looked at pictures of Elizabeth that Andrew had given my mother. I was surprised about how alike we all were, although I knew that I shouldn't have been. I looked at pictures of us with our brother, Joshua - the brother who had stood in front of our real mother to save her life. His selflessness reminded me strongly of Emma. I realised now that perhaps Emma's attitude towards others had actually come from our birth mother, though there was no doubt that it was further strengthened by the wonderful childhoods we had come to live, with the only parents that I had ever known.

It was a lot to take in. I felt sad that my parents and brother had been taken from me so cruelly, yet glad that my mother's family had come to the decisions that they had. I'm not saying that I thought Robert was right for killing Ian because I don't believe in an eye for an eye, but I did feel that Elizabeth's family, my family, had come right in the end. They had done the right thing by her in her death, even if they hadn't been perfect to her when she was alive.

I was looking forward to meeting the family eventually – my uncle, his wife, and his son, my cousin. I wasn't worried about how they would respond to me. They had shown real kindness to my Mum, Mary. She wasn't part of their family by blood, but I knew that from the way she spoke about Andrew, he welcomed her into it as if she was. I could tell from the relief on her face that she was glad that all of this was over. That she didn't have to worry at night about who might be out there to hurt us and, quite probably, it was a relief for her to know that we were loved. That we had been placed with them out of love, and not neglect, as she had always feared we had.

I put the photographs on my kitchen fridge as I started to have a quick tidy around. I called Emma's friend, Hannah, to see how the children were doing. I felt guilty for not being there for them, but I knew that Emma would understand. I couldn't be everywhere all at once and I had been worried about Mum and this wild goose chase with Edd to Chester. Hannah had always been good with the children. I liked her; she'd been a good friend to Emma. I could talk to her as if she were my own close, childhood friend, though that was hardly surprising given the amount of time she had spent in our house, playing when we were growing up.

While I was putting the washing away, I heard the phone ring downstairs. As I was walking to answer it, I was thinking about how good it was going to be to see Emma that evening and tell her all about our biological parents. I was wondering if I might even get a response from her. I felt like she was beginning to become stronger, although the doctors disagreed. It happens though, doesn't it? People wake up after years and years of being in a coma. They go back to life as if everything was just the same, as if the coma had never happened. Perhaps it was a pipe dream to believe that the same thing could be true for Emma. But I wanted to believe it; I had to believe it. If we all just gave up hope then it was admitting defeat. Admitting that Emma was already gone.

"Hello?" I said.

"Sophie Evans?" the voice asked.

"Yes, that's me," I replied, a little shakily, wondering who was calling. The voice seemed familiar to me, but it wasn't one that I could recognise instantly.

"It's Mr. Abraham from Preston Royal Infirmary. I'm afraid that Emma has taken a turn for the worse. I recommend that you come down immediately...."

I flung the phone down onto the floor before I listened to him any further. I grabbed my car keys and coat, and set off to Preston without a second thought.

*

As I walked into the ICU, the nurse on the desk gestured for me to go in the family room. I could see that there were several doctors around Emma's bedside. My parents sat in one corner of the room. James sat to one side of them, while Hannah sat on the other, with Finn on her lap and Poppy sitting beside her. There was something about the distance between Hannah and James that seemed odd, but I didn't have the time to ponder it.

Poppy jumped from Hannah's knee and came towards me. I picked her up and hugged her, shooting a look at Hannah. Why had they brought the children here? Why had they thought that bringing a six and four-year-old to their mother's deathbed was a good idea? Hannah gestured to James, who shrugged his shoulders. Emma had been four years old when our mother had died. Though, admittedly, in very different circumstances. Sadly, it was history repeating itself, almost.

After around five minutes, Mr. Abraham came in.

"Emma has started to experience multiple organ failure. I'm afraid that there's little we can do, and anything that we could do can only extend her life shortly but you would really have to ask yourselves if it was the kind of life that you would want her to live."

"How long have we got left?" James asked him.

"I estimate a few hours - a day at most - kept like this. The kindest thing would be to have some time with her, and then turn off the ventilator. She will just slip peacefully away," Mr. Abraham answered.

"James, it's time to decide," my mother said to him, softly.

A silence filled the room. We all knew what James was thinking. We all loved Emma. But how easy would it be to say the words out loud? To admit to the world that it was time to let her go. Life was for living - for warm summer days, watching chicks grow, crunching leaves beneath your feet in the autumn, finding the biggest hill to sledge down, baking chocolate brownies. Emma wasn't living, not like this. But how would we all cope without her?

I looked around the room. Silent tears were falling down everyone's cheeks. We all knew that it was the right thing to do. But it just felt so heartbreakingly bad. It had to be James's decision. He would be the one who would sit down with the children one day, when they were grown up, and tell them all about their mother. I thought of Millie, the same age I was when I lost Elizabeth. She would never remember Emma. Never remember her kind voice, the soft smell of her perfume. We would have to all work hard to talk about her to the children without sadness tainting our voices. The path ahead would be difficult.

Eventually, James spoke.

"It's time to let her go," he said.

Chapter Thirty Eight

<u>James</u>

What can I say, in all honesty, about that day? About the day I prepared to say goodbye to the woman I loved the most – my best friend, my lover, my soul-mate. The woman who had made my world perfect.

I understood now the pain of having to say goodbye to someone before it was their time. It makes it all even more unbearable than it already was. I remembered saying goodbye to my grandparents when I was a little boy. They had lived long and full lives and, sad as it was, their time had come. Since the day of Emma's accident, I had always known that this day might come – though, I had always tried hard to believe that it wouldn't. I was not emotionally prepared, not ready to say goodbye to her – but then could you ever be?

As the others went in, one by one, to say goodbye to Emma – her mother, her father, her best-friend, her sister, and her daughter, I reflected on the life that we had lived together as husband and wife. I wasn't a martyr, and I wasn't going to say that our lives had been utterly perfect. Of course, we had our ups and downs - the same as everyone else. Of course there were things about Emma that irritated me slightly – the way she seemed to get water all over the bathroom after she'd had a bath, the way she had forgotten to take off her outdoor shoes after shutting the hens in and got mud all over the kitchen floor. They didn't matter though, the little things. They didn't make Emma any less than she already was. I thought about the little things that Emma did, for me and our children. The way that she made cakes in the afternoons when no one was around and we were busy with our own lives, she hid them from us as we returned from work and school, and slid them into our lunchboxes the next day. The way that she talked to the children as if she had endless time and endless patience. How would we ever live without her?

I'd brought Poppy and Finn here on a gut instinct. I knew that if this was really it, then they ought to be able to say goodbye to their mother. Were they too young? Would this cause them long-term psychological damage? I was no expert. But I knew that this would help them to understand. I couldn't sit down and tell them that their mother had died. They would never understand it, not properly. It may seem cruel and heartless, but what choice did I really have? They had to deal with their loss, just the same as everyone else.

Eventually, after all the others had been to see Emma, and came back with tear-soaked clothing and eyes that were red raw, it was my turn. I walked into the ICU for what would be the last time.

Emma lay, as she always was, on her back. Her hair was plaited loosely, the hospital gown hung off her frail body. She'd lost a fair amount of weight while she had been in the hospital, her skin clung to her cheekbones, and she'd lost her glow. I stroked her hair and watched her for a while. She still looked so beautiful. She was too young to die like this. Too young to leave her family behind.

"Oh, Emma," I said to her.

"You were always so strong in spirit, so determined to do things your own way. But it's too late. Your body is giving up on you, bit by bit. They've tried to bring you back, wean you off the ventilator, but you're just so weak...there's nothing else that they can do now. You'll be better off moving on – looking after Iris, watching over us. It's going to be hard, Emma, It's going to be so hard to live without you. I'm not sure that I can manage the children by myself; I don't have the patience that you have, and I don't always know how to encourage them to be themselves. But you know that I'll do my best, that I'll never let them forget you. I'll tell them all the stories of us, of the times that we did things together. I've got to soldier on because of them, haven't I? I've got to make sure that they remember you, every single day, every school exam, and every driving test. I don't want them to forget you; I don't want you to become a distant memory to them.

"I feel like my heart is shattered into a thousand pieces. I want to be with you; I want you to be with us. I should have known that something bad had happened to you that night; I should have gone looking. I'm sorry that I let you down, Emma. I'm sorry that we can't do anything else for you now. Letting go of you, Emma, is the hardest thing I've ever had to do. But you're already gone from us, now. You've already moved on, haven't you? You're already at peace."

I closed my eyes for a moment and let the tears flow down my face. I didn't bother wiping them away, didn't bother trying to hide my grief.

I felt a soft hand on my right shoulder, and looked to see Mr. Abraham standing beside me.

"It is time," he said, softly.

I nodded my head, and was amazed to see my family standing behind him. All of the people that Emma had loved with her whole heart. All of the people that wouldn't let her go on her own, who would be there with her until her very last breath.

Mr. Abraham nodded to another doctor. They were going to turn off the ventilator. They had given her what they could to make her comfortable, though, in her current unconscious state, she would feel no pain. She would pass away within a few minutes. Mr. Abraham and his colleague stepped back.

I held her hand; I buried my face in her nightgown. I tried to stop myself from breaking down on the outside as I was within. I had to be strong now; I had to be strong for Emma. She couldn't be afraid. I felt as someone came and grabbed my right hand and gave it a soft squeeze. The gesture of kindness gave me a chance to gulp back my sobs. When I looked up through my tears, I saw that everyone was standing around her bedside, hand in hand. It was the most beautiful moment - no less than Emma deserved.

The machines started to protest as her vital statistics started dropping.

I felt a calming presence floating all around the room.
I told Emma that we loved her.
Just like that, she was gone.

Chapter Thirty Nine

Hannah

We all left the hospital that evening with heavy hearts. James had to stay behind to fill in some paperwork, so I offered to take the children, pick up Millie from James's parents and head back to the house.

Poppy and Finn were quiet on the journey home, the quietest that I think I'd ever heard them. They sat, stone-faced, all the way back to the Lake District. I didn't have the right words to ease their pain. I couldn't take it away from them, just as I couldn't take away my own. We had all lost someone very special in our lives, and it would take us all time to heal. I knew that the next few days would be hard on us all.

Millie was her usual self as I picked her up, giggling happily and babbling away. I clipped her into the car and took the bag of cooked food that James's mother offered to me – some kind of casserole, and mashed potatoes in a separate plastic tub. I was grateful for her small act of kindness to us, although I knew, really, that she was doing it for James and the children. I hadn't even thought about food - although I realised that there hadn't been much in the kitchen this morning, when I went to make the children their breakfast.

We arrived home and collapsed on the sofa. Finn put on children's TV, and I was grateful for the distraction. I looked around at the photographs that were all over the living room of Emma, Emma and James, Emma and the children. The reality of her dying was beginning to sink in. She would never sit in this living room again. We would never have our Sunday night catch-ups. She'd never be able to walk the children to school, watch Poppy in her ballet shows, or see Millie's first steps.

I put the casserole in the oven and poured myself a glass of red wine. I disconnected the landline. I didn't think that I could bear to answer the phone at a time like this. James returned a little later; the children at least became a little more animated and a little more back to normal.

We talked about what would happen next, about the funeral arrangements and all the calls that had to be made. Poppy and Finn had two more days left at school, and James thought it would do them good to get out of the house, to carry on as normal. I'd already called work and taken some compassionate leave. Christmas was a week away, they didn't need me there, and I couldn't carry on booking holidays for people as if the world were a wonderful and happy place.

Mary and Bob thought that Emma would have wanted to have her service at the Kingdom Hall. Although it wasn't where she and James had married since he had been a non-believer. It seemed so long ago now, the wedding – the happiest day of Emma's life. Mary and Bob were going to talk to the other Witnesses and ask their permission, because, as a lapsed Witness, a funeral at the Kingdom Hall wasn't automatic. There were procedures to follow. James had insisted that Emma should be buried in the churchyard in Ambleside, St. Mary's. So that her grave was more accessible to the children as they grew up. Somehow, he had found the strength to phone the relevant people in Manchester to see if it were possible for Iris's tiny body to be moved. James was right; it was what Emma would have wanted.

Between us, we bathed and tucked the children in bed. Poppy and Finn seemed accepting of Emma's death. There were no awkward questions, no asking why. Millie had stopped asking for Emma after the first week or so of the accident. For her, it was as if her mother had already been long-gone.

James joined me on the sofa, and we sat saying nothing, staring at the flames in the log burner.

"I'm sorry, Hannah, you know, for the other night. For not saying and doing the right things. It's all just been..." James began.

"Please, don't. It's all forgotten now. Immaterial. There's more important things that we need to focus on..." I let my voice trail off as I began to think about organising the funeral – sending out invitations, organising a caterer. There were so many things to sort out.

"Maybe it would be best if you went home?" James asked me. I studied his face. He wasn't saying it out of anger, out of a desperate need to shut me away and forget that I existed. He needed time and space to deal with his pain, to look after his children.

"Now that Emma's really gone, well, I need to get used to looking after the children by myself. You can't be here forever. You don't owe me that – you have your own life to live, Hannah. If this has taught me one thing...you can't waste anything. Not a second of what time, you have left. The children will be fine. I'll be fine. But you don't need to be dragged down by this; you don't need to be responsible for picking up the pieces. That's my job now."

I nodded at him.

"You'll call me though, won't you? If you need anything. You'll let me come and see the children?"

"Of course."

"Don't be a stranger, James. Don't let your grief weigh you down."

"I'll try my best," he replied.

Chapter Forty

Edd

So many things had changed in such a short amount of time.

The most significant thing for me had been the police's sudden interest in the accident since Emma had died. Suddenly, they wanted to listen to James, to talk to Mary and Bob about their daughter. As if all the time that she'd been lying in the hospital didn't matter because she'd been alive then. As if they were only going to pretend to be interested when they had to. People were talking, you see, and not in a good way. Emma had been murdered. She had been liked and loved by so many in the community; she was kind to strangers; she got involved in charity events. Her death didn't make sense. Quite rightly, people wanted someone to be held responsible. They wanted to know that whoever had hurt Emma that day, wasn't going to come looking for their next victim.

With all of the emotions flying around after that dreadful afternoon, I went home for a few days. Mary and Bob needed space, James was snowed under, and Sophie was trying to deal with the loss of her sister and gaining a family that she never knew existed. It was a trying time for Emma's family, and I was grateful to go home and take a breather. Grateful to be able to spend time with

Sarah and pop in on Alan. It's so easy, isn't it, to take for granted things that are normal?

I went through all of the information that James had gleaned about Iris and Joe. I had to hand it to him - he'd done a very good job. I made sure that a copy of Iris's autopsy was sent to the caseworker that was dealing with Joe and Rachel's filing for custody of Poppy. It seemed unlikely now that the court would go in his favour, although it had all gone quiet on that front. I wondered how long it would take until James was given full custody, and I sincerely hoped it wouldn't be long.

The funeral had been arranged for Christmas Eve, which seemed like a strange day to me. Although, obviously, Christmas wasn't a factor for Mary and Bob. It would be held at the Kingdom Hall and there would be tea and cake afterwards at a nearby hotel. I knew that James had celebrated Christmas while they were married, so I imagined that at least Christmas the following day would perhaps take away some of the pain for the children; although, it would take a long time for them to heal properly.

I'd been going through the list of people that Emma knew, with meticulous detail. Sarah would moan as she went to bed herself most evenings, but I had very little choice. I wanted to work out who all of these people on the list were so that I could place them all when I attended Emma's funeral. I'd asked Mary for photographs before I had left. I wanted to be able to pick off anyone who wasn't on the list, or anyone who was acting strangely.

My time working for the police had taught me many things. But the one thing that always stood in my mind was this; a murderer appears at a victim's funeral in 99% of all investigations.

I wasn't usually one to count my chickens before they had hatched, but I had a hunch that in a few days' time I would be looking into the eyes of the person who was responsible for Emma's death, and I had to be prepared.

Chapter Forty One

Mary

How can I explain the pain of losing my daughter? The gut-wrenching feeling that followed me everywhere I went. The brief moments when I would think of Emma in the present, when I would think to tell her that Lakeland Limited was having a sale and then realise, all over again, that she's gone. It doesn't matter how many times it happens; it doesn't make the ache any less.

Bob has been better than me at hiding his grief. At getting on with his life. He could say all the right things to people, when they stopped us in the street to pass on their condolences. *'She couldn't go on like that,'* he would say or *'We will find peace, when the time is right'*. I would just stand beside him.

I've thrown myself into organising the funeral arrangements. We have been given permission to hold the service at the hall, which is a great relief to me. I know that it's what Emma would have wanted. When she was younger, she had such a strong faith. The Kingdom Hall had been where she and James had married.

People in the congregation have been calling to offer their help, and I had forgotten how being a Witness could bring such comfort in difficult times. How people think about the small things. One of the sisters was a florist, another was a cake maker.

Between them, they offered to decorate the hall and make little cakes, vanilla cupcakes, which were always Emma's favourite, for people to take as they left.

Afterwards, James had booked a local hotel just outside Ambleside for an afternoon tea. When Bob had gone up to pay the bill two days before the funeral the manager shook his head and told him it had already been settled. What did such a big hotel owe us? They hadn't known Emma personally. Such small acts of kindness were what helped us get through this difficult time.

As I carried on making all of the arrangements, I tried not to think about what we would soon be going through. It isn't right for parents to be burying their daughter; it's not the way that it should be. It was going to take a lot of strength to get through the funeral.

James has been coping remarkably well. I know that like us, he suffers with the loss of Emma every day. He sees her in little ways in the children. Sophie had gone round to help him with Emma's things - her clothes, her perfumes, and her jewellery. They packed them up and put some of it in the loft for the children to see when they were old enough. They sent her clothes to the local charity shop. Sophie had told us afterwards that it seemed cruel; tossing all of her things into black bin bags, but that it was the kindest thing to do for James. He could not be reminded of his loss every time he opened the wardrobe, or the bathroom cupboard. He had to go on living, like the rest of us, without Emma.

Andrew Cook and his wife would be coming to the house tomorrow. He wanted to be at the funeral, and Bob suggested that he came up before, so that it wasn't yet another thing for Sophie to be worrying about when there were already going to be emotions running high. Andrew was a kind man. I was sure that he and Sophie would get on well, but it was a great shame that he had never been reacquainted with Emma again.

Edd was getting ready to resume his investigations after the funeral. We all agreed that we had to carry on looking for Emma's killer. That we wouldn't really be able to find closure until the person responsible was found – until justice had been sought.

It was five days until the funeral.

It was five days until we would be letting go of Emma.

Would our lives ever be the same again?

Chapter Forty Two

<u>Sophie</u>

As the days slipped by without Emma, life began to have a new pattern.

Most days, I would pop over to James's and make sure that he and the children were okay – I'd take the children to Rufty Tufty's for an hour, to let him have some space and let them run off some steam. I also started to do normal things – I went to the supermarket for food, went for a walk along the river, went to meet up with friends as if everything was normal and I hadn't just lost my sister, my best friend. Every day things seemed to get a little easier, as the anger of Emma's death began shifting to acceptance.

Those first few days without her were a haze of pain and I shut myself away, became lost in my grief. We were all numb and speechless. What words could we say that would make it all okay? What could we do to take away each other's pain? We were all suffering in our own way. We all had to try to move forward as best as we could. Emma wouldn't have wanted us to be like this. Emma would have wanted us to go on living.

Andrew Cook and his wife were coming to visit me later this morning. I was nervous about meeting my uncle, the first meeting I would have with anyone who I was related to by blood for a long time. Yet, I knew that my mother's instincts about other people were usually right. He had, after all, shown great courage and compassion for acting as he had on that day that my real mother, Elizabeth, and my brother had been shot by Ian. He had put the needs of us, his sister's children, before his own. He and my grandfather had made sure that we were safe, and loved. Most importantly, it was their actions, on that day, that meant that we were given to Mary and Bob. For that, there could never be enough words of thanks. We had been given so many things, not materialistic things - the ability to love others, to care for people, to do the right thing. We had been shown the act of forgiveness.

For all of our childhood, Emma had never been interested in finding our birth parents. When I tried to talk to her about it, she would say that I should let it go, that Mary and Bob loved us, that raking up the past would only hurt them as much as it would hurt me. I wondered now if subconsciously, she had known that they were dead all along. She had been much older than me the day that Andrew found us in the wardrobe. She would have heard the gunshots. Perhaps forgetting had been her way of coping, her way of moving on? We would never know now. It was a shame that Emma had died without knowing the truth. A shame that she had never lived to be reunited with our family.

A soft knock on the door interrupted my thoughts, and I walked over to open it. Andrew and his wife, Clare, looked up at me. I was shocked by the familiarity of his face, as if he were an old, lost friend.

"Sophie...you've changed so much...." he said to me. I could feel my eyes filling with tears as he moved forwards to hug me.

"You really are your mother's daughter," he said as he stepped back, looking at me, smiling gently. I nodded. My mother brought back some pictures of Elizabeth and Joshua, and we had shared them, over tea, the day before we lost Emma. Both Emma and I had grown up to look very like her.

"Come in," I told them, standing aside. "The kettle's just boiled. We've got a lot of catching up to do."

Chapter Forty Three

James

The day before Emma's funeral, Christmas Eve's eve, we were sitting around the house. It was, by all other standards, just a normal day. Poppy and Finn wanted to put up the Christmas tree, which was something that I seemed to have been putting off. We headed over to the garden centre to pick up a real tree and they bickered about which one was really the best. I paid, threw it into the back of the car, and was just juggling the three children and the tree when I saw Joe's wife walking up towards the house. I told Poppy and Finn to go inside and handed her Millie.

"If you're here, you may as well make yourself useful," I said, grabbing the tree and closing the car boot. Poppy had been due at the contact centre two days after Emma had gone. I didn't take her. It didn't seem fair, didn't seem right that on top of dealing with the loss of her mother she should be forced to play happy families with someone else. I had called Poppy's caseworker and she had been cold and unsympathetic. She had advised me against it. I had told her that it was not up for negotiation. That if I ended up in court then I would explain it to a judge if I had to.

"Is this about Saturday?" I asked her, putting the tree down in the porch and taking Millie back from her.

"No. I was hoping that we could talk? I know it's a lot to ask..."

I looked up at her. What did I really have to lose?

"Come on, I'll put the kettle on," I said, gesturing for her to follow me. I put Millie down on the carpet next to Poppy and Finn, who were playing with Finn's wooden train set, went into the kitchen, and switched the kettle on.

"Joe and I have separated," she said. I wasn't surprised.

"Emma's gone," I replied.

A silence filled the kitchen. I made two cups of tea and put them down on the table.

"I didn't know... about Iris."

"I didn't know either, not until after the accident." Rachel looked up at me.

"Emma was a wonderful woman, but she wasn't perfect. Losing Iris was probably the most difficult time in her life. There are certain things that are difficult to talk about. Certain things that just seem cruel and unfair..."

"I realised that Joe wasn't who I thought he was. He wasn't the man that I thought I had married. He didn't see how this changed everything. He thought that Poppy was a toy, something that he could have, now that he wanted her, something that he could throw away when he didn't."

"Did you never wonder why he didn't love her? How he could shut his own daughter out?" I asked her. It had been something that both Emma and I had never understood. Not only Joe's complete lack of interest, but also the way in which another woman could just understand and accept it. Surely, on some subconscious level, she must have thought that Joe could have done the same thing to her? He had done it to one woman; he was certainly capable of doing it to another.

"I believed his lies. That Emma had decided to keep the baby, that she had moved away, which made it difficult. He told me that once Emma and you were together, it made things even more difficult for him to see Poppy."

I should have guessed that he hadn't told Rachel the truth. Why would he? He would have hardly come out of the situation in a favourable light. It was hardly something that you wanted people to think, is it? That you had a daughter that you didn't ever give more than a passing thought?

"Emma never stopped Joe from seeing Poppy, although I often thought that she should have done. All he did, when she was small, was confuse her – disappear for months on end and then turn up out of the blue. When Emma and I were engaged, she decided that she wasn't going to call him anymore. She wasn't going to remind him to send her a birthday card, or ask when he was coming to see her. Joe had to want to do it for himself, and if he didn't, then Emma thought it was probably best if he didn't have as much contact with Poppy. Predictably, he used it as an excuse. He blamed anyone other than himself. He probably told himself that it was better this way. Better to have a little girl grow up knowing that her father cares so little about her that she isn't even worth a birthday card."

"Joe didn't want Poppy because he thought that he *should* be the one to look after her when Emma was ill. He saw it as a way to give me what I wanted. He thought that if we had Poppy, then our problems would just disappear. But they wouldn't. We talked about Poppy after that first contact session. She's such a lovely little girl. But Joe was relieved to hand her back. He didn't have anything to say to her, didn't see that she was just a little girl who might have other wants and needs. She was talking about you, and Joe stepped in, he told her that you weren't her father," Rachel said.

"That's because in Joe's mind I'm not. He thinks' that blood is more important than actually being a father. He thinks' that he can do what he likes, when he likes, and that he will still have the upper-hand over all of us. The thing is, legally he's right. Biological fathers have more rights than ever."

"I told Joe that we can't take Poppy like that, but I began to believe him. I began to think that she would be better off having regular contact with Joe. That she might get something out of her relationship with him that she doesn't get from you. But I was wrong. In light of our separation, they will withdraw our request for custody. They'll stop all of the contacts. Joe doesn't want Poppy; he never has. They'll give her to you, legally. She can carry on living the life that she has always known."

I was touched by Rachel's kindness. She didn't owe me anything. She didn't have to come here, miles out of her way, to tell me all of this. She could have waited for me to hear it from the caseworker. She could have left, like Joe had left Poppy all of those years ago – without a backwards glance.

"Thank you," I said. She smiled. "What about you, what will you do now?" I asked her.

"I'll take him to the cleaners and then? I'll move on, find someone else eventually. I can adopt, one day. Adopt a child who really does have nothing, instead of taking away a child from having everything that she could ever want."

I admired her resilience. It took a lot of courage to walk away from someone when something wasn't right. A lot of courage to admit that she had made a bad choice. So many people stayed in bad situations because they thought that they owed it to their husbands, that they would disappoint their fathers.

Rachel stood up to leave and I followed her to the front door.

"I hope that you can find peace sometime soon, James, that you'll become free from the pain of losing Emma. Poppy does have a wonderful father. You've given her everything. You love her as if she were your own. Poppy deserves the best now, and the best is you, James."

I watched her as she walked back down the drive. Bit by bit, things were coming right. As I turned to go back inside to my children, I picked up the tree and dragged it into the living room. Emma would want us to go on. Tomorrow would be a difficult day for all of us, but at least we had each other.

Chapter Forty Four

<u>Hannah</u>

I arrived at the Kingdom Hall early. It was filled with beautiful white lilies. I had decided not to follow the funeral car from the morgue. I wanted to hand out the order of services, give the vicar the USB of songs that Mary and James had decided to play as people were leaving the church. I wanted to be there as people came in, to talk about little things that weren't important. To see that I wasn't the only one who was suffering.

The Kingdom Hall began to fill very quickly, which wasn't really surprising. Emma knew a lot of people and it was times like this that the community rallied together and looked after its own. Everyone who had known Emma had turned out – had taken unpaid days off work, had cancelled all other plans with their families.

As I stood waiting outside for the funeral car, it arrived slowly and cautiously, along the road. The reality of the day began to dawn on me and I felt my eyes start to form soft tears that glided down my face.

Emma was going to be buried in a white coffin and I was struck by its beauty. Two flower arrangements lay on the top, saying 'Mum' and 'wife'. I tried to hold back the tears. I tried to stay focused.

James, the children, Mary, Bob, and Sophie came from the cars behind it. James handed me Millie and nodded to me.

"We can do this, Hannah. We've got to be strong, for the children," he told me.

He was right.

As the bearers lifted the coffin, we followed it silently and found our seats in the front row. As the speaker began to talk about Emma, I thought about the things we had done as children, then as teenagers. About the things we had done as young women. She'd been there for me always, a phone call away. So many different people would miss her in so many different ways.

Bob read a section of The Bible before some music played for a few minutes. Poppy and Finn walked up to the coffin and put letters on the top of it. It was so heartbreakingly wrong.

James stood up to speak.

"So many of you knew Emma and loved her in your own ways. What can I say that you haven't already thought? That you haven't already heard? We never spoke much, Emma and I, about what would happen on this day. Why would we? Emma was so young and had many more years ahead of her. Dying is something that should happen when your body is old and tired, not when it is still young and full of life. We asked you today to wear bright colours, because we can't be sad forever, Emma wouldn't have wanted that. Although there are still things about the accident that don't make sense to us now, one day, we will have all the answers. Together, we can move forward and remember

Emma how she would want to be remembered - as a wonderful woman, a good friend, and neighbour, as someone who cared as much for others as she cared about herself and her family. Emma was loyal, faithful, and kind. She had a wonderful life with so many different opportunities and she will be greatly missed by all of us. I'm going to leave you with a slideshow that Sophie has put together of Emma's life."

As the slideshow began to play, I could hear the soft sobs of people in the congregation. The images flicked from a picture of Emma, Sophie, and their older brother to the time just after Mary and Bob had adopted them. From her early childhood to her teens, and up through to the present day – the life that she had lived with James and the children. It was a beautiful compilation.

As I looked around, there was not a dry eye in the house. As the coffin was carried back out of the Kingdom Hall and put back into the funeral car for its final journey to the graveyard in Ambleside. James handed Poppy and Finn two white doves, and he held the third with Millie.

We watched as they let go of the birds and they flew high towards the clouds and left us. The sky was beginning to break. As cold as it was, the sun peaked through the clouds. As if Emma were looking down on all of us.

I whispered my goodbyes to her in that moment, just as the people started to leave. I held Poppy's hand tightly.

There were only ten of us going back to the graveyard, before the wake began. One more task for us to complete together, and then that would be it. Emma would be gone.

Chapter Forty Five

<u>Sophie</u>

We followed the funeral car back to Ambleside, a journey that I made often. Today though, time seemed to stand still – every second seemed longer than the last. We stood around while they lowered the coffin deep into the ground. I held on to my mother's arm more tightly than I normally would. I could feel her pain seeping out of her, as it was for all of us. The local vicar had come to say a few words. They placed Iris's tiny coffin on top of Emma's. We all threw in handfuls of dirt.

I took one last look at the coffins before I turned away. It was over. This is how my life would be from now on. No sister to look up to and protect me. I thought fleetingly about Joshua and the cruel ending to his life. Both of my siblings were now gone. I would have to make sure I lived my life for both of them.

Leaving James, to have his last moment with Emma, we walked back to the cars, which were parked in the churchyard car park. The wake was at a local hotel. Is it bad that what I wanted most in that moment was to go home, alone? Is it bad that the last thing that I really wanted to do right now was to go and talk to people about Emma? If it hadn't have been for the children and my parents, I probably would have just left. I would have remembered Emma in my own way. I'd have eaten a large piece of cake, had a large glass of wine, and had an early night.

The hotel was just outside of the village, overlooking the lake. Mum and James had chosen it because it had always been one of Emma's favourite places to go. I don't think that any of us could have coped with having it at the house. The Kingdom Hall had been packed; if even half of them came to the hotel, then it would be cosy indeed.

The staff at the hotel were lovely, taking coats, offering drinks. Cakes were piled high on tables all over the room. People seemed to be taking one and chattering away in small groups. I managed to retreat into a side room where I found my Mum and the children. Mum looked like she had aged years in this one day. Her eyes were raw and pinched – her lack of sleep in recent nights was plainly obvious.

"It'll get easier, won't it?" I asked her.

"Of course it will. Time can be a great healer." She managed a smile. I watched the children play with some Lego on the floor. Millie was asleep in her pushchair. I grabbed a piece of Victoria sponge and washed it down with my tea. I glanced around to see a lot of familiar faces from over the years – our neighbours from when we had been little girls, our schoolteachers, our friends. Emma would have been astonished about the amount of people who had turned out today.

Hannah came and sat by me on the sofa. We chatted idly about not a lot, about the weather, our holiday plans. I knew that Hannah had recently split up with her long-term partner, Jim. Mum told me that she had handed in her notice at work, that she couldn't cope with working at the moment. I could understand it perfectly well. Doing normal things while Emma had been ill had phased me for a long time. Hannah and Emma had been very close for a number of years. I made a mental note to make sure that I remembered to call Hannah from time to time, check in on her and make sure that everything was okay. I had my own friends, my own life without Emma. People I could talk to. Hannah and Emma were like two peas in a pod. Suddenly, Hannah was left in an empty shell.

  I stood up and went for a wander around, nodding at people in the right places. Saying hello to people that recognised me. I noticed Edd talking to a man that I didn't recognise, near the window overlooking Lake Windermere. They seemed deep in conversation. On the other side of the room, my Dad was talking to the old head teacher of Ambleside Primary School. He'd long since retired, but I knew that he thought fondly of all his ex-pupils, and he still lived in the village.

  People had started to leave in dribs and drabs. I was grateful that as the crowds started to disappear, people started being more like themselves. Poppy and Finn were now running around playing with balloons. I'd soon become tired of the disapproving looks from elderly people who had come to pay their respects. Of course, I understood that maybe it didn't seem right, but they were just children. Children who had just lost their mother. I wasn't going to take that tiny moment of happiness away from them. I wasn't going to scold them and tell them to go and sit down quietly, with more glum expressions. They would feel the pain of their mothers' death for long enough. They would be reminded of her absence for the rest of their lives.

I walked up to the bar and stood next to James, who was nursing something strong in a glass. I ordered a large glass of wine.

"It still doesn't feel right, you know," he said to me. "Her clothes are gone; her things have been put away. But I can still feel her; see her, in every room of the house."

I nodded at him. It must be difficult. Thoughts of Emma came back to me often, but we hadn't lived together since we were children. We hadn't shared things as intimately. I was used to Emma being in my house, but it wasn't unusual for her not to be there either.

"Maybe you should think about moving?" I asked him, gently.

"Yes, I wondered...but I don't want to unsettle the children any more than is needed. You know? I think they've had to cope with enough. Today and tomorrow are going to be difficult for them. They are used to Emma being there for them, in everything they do. Poppy pretends that it doesn't upset her, but I can hear her crying into her pillow at night. I know that Finn doesn't want to go to play with his friend's afterschool anymore, because he is tired of all the questions that people keep asking him; he just wants to be."

"But what do you want, James?" I asked him.

He looked at me as if I were asking the most stupid question in the world. As if I shouldn't even have to ask. I wasn't anticipating his answer. I thought we were talking about moving homes, moving furniture, starting afresh.

"I want Emma back. But that isn't going to happen, is it? So the next best thing? I want to find her killer – I want to find him and ask him *why?* I want to know who he is, what Emma had done to deserve this. I want the answers."

I thought about it for a moment. James was right. We would never be able to move on in our lives with all of this uncertainty hanging over us. I wondered how Edd and his investigations were going. I wondered if they were moving forward at all. I hadn't spoken to my parents about it for fear of upsetting them. I didn't want to ask them in case there was nothing else to know, and often, in case there was. I didn't think that there could be any justifiable reason for whatever happened on that night. I didn't think that whoever had done this should be able to sleep soundly at night in their own beds, while we were all going through this torment.

"Do you think we will ever find them?" I asked James. It was a question that I hadn't dared to ask anyone else.

"We will find them, Sophie. We will find them if I have to keep looking every single day for the rest of my life. I need to be able to look the children in the eyes when they are old enough to understand. I need to give them answers. I will not tell them that we never found out the truth. I will not tell them that I do not have the answers. Emma would have done the same for us. We can't do anything for her now, in life. But this is the one last thing we can do. She would want us to have peace. She would want the children to understand why, to be able to grow up without questions. I don't know how we're going to do it. It's probably going to take all the strength we've got. I'm going to try and keep the holidays normal. I'm going to try and let the children have a break before they go back to school in January. Then after that, I'm going to do whatever I can to help Edd. He's a good bloke. His heart is in the right place. He is sharp, and meticulous. If anyone can find out who did this, it's him."

"Are you sure?" I said looking across at Edd, who was still deep in conversation with the unknown man. I liked Edd. I thought that he had done well to find out so much about our birth parents in such little time. But, like the rest of us, he was getting older. Was he really up to this kind of investigation? Or was he doing it out of a sense of obligation to my father? After all, he could have hardly turned them down after he received their call. He could hardly have said, *'Sorry I'm a bit busy'* and not given it another thought. Edd was in a classic "catch twenty-two" situation. I thought that if anyone other than my mother had called him that day, he would have probably refused. He liked a quiet life now - he didn't work on high-profile cases anymore. But still, perhaps his sense of obligation would make him a better investigator. One that was more determined, one that didn't take no for an answer. I didn't know what he had done to get as far as he had, but certainly, there had been some strings pulled somewhere. Edd had contacts, and he knew how to use them. It would either make or break the investigation, or perhaps both if I thought about it truthfully.

"I'm sure," James replied with certainty, taking another drink that the barman had placed in front of him.

I took a large gulp of my wine. Its bitter taste slid down my throat.

If one thing was right, I knew that we had to face this, together. We were either all on the boat or the boat wouldn't sail. I knew that arriving at our destination wouldn't be easy. That we would have to weather storms, and we might land somewhere else first. But we had to at least try, didn't we?

I looked across the room at Poppy and Finn. They were sitting now, in another window, which was looking out towards the lake. They were doing a puzzle of some kind, trying to find the edge pieces so that the whole thing could eventually come together, that the picture on the pieces would be complete. If nothing else, those children deserved the truth.

We had already begun our puzzle. So many of the bits were now slotted into place. We just had to find order in the rest of them, and fit them all together. Then we would know. In my mind, it seemed so easy. In my mind, I thought that there must have been something that we had all just overlooked.

"Do you have names and numbers for everyone that Emma knew?" I asked him. He nodded glumly.

"I've already tried that." He said in a defeated voice.

"Well, you give me all the notes that you have made. I'll call them all again. Catch them off guard, compare the notes. Only, this time, I'll call on them personally. They are more likely to crack under pressure, right?" James nodded.

"After that, we might be able to see things with a bit more clarity," I told him.

"I hope you're right," he replied.

It was worth a long shot. After all, we had nothing to lose.

PART THREE

Chapter Forty Six

James

It has been one month since I lost my wife. One month since the day that I let her go. The days after her funeral are now blurry. We spent Christmas with my parents at our house, the children were ecstatic with their new toys, the tins of chocolates. I'd found a gift that Emma had carefully wrapped and placed in the loft, weeks before her accident. It was a grey cashmere scarf, so soft to the touch, so delicate. I had a plain scarf that I wore for work when the weather was cold, but it was scruffy, old, and long beyond its best. I kept the scarf in the box in my wardrobe. Some days, I would take it out and touch it. Others I would look at it in disgust and wonder why I had kept it? Things were only just starting to feel a bit more normal. I was a long way off returning to work.

The good things that had happened since Emma had gone? Well, there was only one thing that I could think of: Joe had removed his attempt at fighting for custody of Poppy, as predicted. The family courts had legally entrusted me as her guardian. We were still filling out all of the papers for the adoption, but that wouldn't take long now. I wouldn't take another penny off Joe in child maintenance payments. The money that he had provided for Poppy in the past now seemed insignificant. We didn't need it. I didn't need him coming back, years later, with his claim that, if nothing else, he had always been there for her financially. Poppy deserved better than that.

For the past month, Sophie had been calling on everyone that Emma had ever known. We met in the evenings to talk about what she had found. Edd had complex diagrams in which every person had a place. But still, all of our efforts had led to nothing. There was no light-bulb moment, nothing that jumped out at us as glaringly obvious. Everyone was accounted for. We were going to have to start looking outside the box if we were ever going to find the answers that we so desperately sought.

Every few days, Hannah would stop by the house. She would take the children out, return them, and politely leave. It saddened me that our friendship had come to this, but I didn't have the strength to deal with something else right now. I couldn't be weighed down with other people's problems when I already had so many of my own. It seemed cruel, I know, but what else could I do? Hannah was a grown woman who was old enough to accept responsibility for her own actions. I know that she missed Emma every day. But I couldn't ease her pain any more than I could ease my own. Hannah needed comfort and love, but I couldn't be the one who gave it to her. Wallowing in the past wasn't going to help either of us. I was now a single father to three small children. I was worried about Mary, who seemed to have become more and more of a social recluse. It wasn't like her and she needed help. Bob insisted that she would find her way through her grief, eventually. But I thought that she needed real help – medication to numb her pain. I had enough to deal with without adding Hannah into the equation.

As I walked into Ambleside and dropped off the children at the school and nursery, I returned to my empty house. Washing needed to be done, the hens needed cleaning out. Life had become an endless circle of jobs. As I unlocked the front door, I noticed that a note lay on the doormat. It was, I thought, far too early for the postman. I picked up the note and started to read.

"I will meet you at 8pm at the stepping stones tonight. I have information about someone who I believe may have hurt your wife."

I stared at the note. Could this be true, or was it just someone seeking attention? Could somebody really know what had happened to Emma?

I knew, right there and then that there was no way I was not going to turn up at the stepping stones later that evening. But I had to be prepared.

I picked up my mobile and called Edd.

Chapter Forty Seven

Mary

As the holiday season turned into a New Year, the pain of losing Emma remained in the background wherever we went. Bob and I carried on as best as we could. But I know that I felt the loss of losing our daughter day-to-day more than Bob. Or at least, I found my pain was far more difficult to hide. Bob was better at getting on with things, at not letting things get him down. He had always been more upbeat than me. He could turn anything negative into a positive. It was something that I had once admired, but now I wondered if it was really right. How could losing your daughter be a positive thing? How could it be what Jehovah had wanted?

Over the holiday season, I went to the Kingdom Hall more often than usual. I went out on my ministry work, because I found peace in it, comfort in the distractions of being busy. Yet, inside, I too was struggling. I felt like I had been let down. I felt that Jehovah had taken away Emma in an act...an act that was quite cruel – an act that left behind three small children without a mother.

When I was a child, my father had often spoken to us about strengthening our faith. He was a man who seemed to have the right answers to everything. He told us often that the firmness of the tree was dependent on the strength of its roots. That if the roots went deep enough, the tree would never be able to fall. He told us that a strong faith had very deep roots, which were strong enough to weather any passing storm. He told us that in difficult times having such strong roots would allow us to draw closer to Jehovah, and that we had to stop evil from getting inside our families. As a child, I had often misinterpreted my father's analogies, but, as an adult, they allowed me to see many things in a different light.

Losing Emma would either tear our family apart or it would strengthen it. We could let it blow us down, or we would remain standing tall. The road ahead was not going to be easy, but we had a choice. We had a choice to sink or swim. It made me think about what Emma would want? That much was obvious. Emma would have wanted us to remember the good times, but to move on with our lives. We had to soldier on. We had to carry on living, because what was the alternative?

It was early evening now. Bob and I had eaten lunch out in town, in a little café, which was just off the main square, which was a rare treat. We had wandered back home along the river and talked about where we might go on holiday later on in the year, about where we might take the grandchildren on a daytrip.

James had called us just after we got back to ask if I could come and watch the children for a couple of hours that evening, and I had agreed without hesitation. I knew that James was as worried for Bob and I as we had been recently for him.

I've had to try hard to step back and give James and the children the space that they needed to move on, which was difficult, because my instinct had been to be there every day, showering them with love. I've refrained from popping over to help with the cleaning, from dropping off meals. I knew that James knew where we were if he needed us. He knew that we would love to help with the children. But equally, he needed to stand on his own two feet. He needs to do what he thinks is best for his family, without having to answer to anyone else or worry about what anyone else might be thinking.

When I arrived at the house just after six o'clock, the children were already fed, bathed, and in their pyjamas. James was uneasy, looking around as if he had misplaced something. I hadn't asked him where he was going, on the phone. I did not want him to feel that he had to justify his actions to us. Just because Emma was gone, it didn't mean we were no longer a family. Just because Emma was gone, shouldn't mean that James wouldn't ever have the chance of happiness again, though I did shudder slightly at the thought of Emma being replaced. Surely, it was far too soon for that?

"So, Poppy and Finn need to read their reading books before bed. Finn has a spelling test tomorrow. There's some cake in the fridge," James said, kissing each of the children and putting on his coat.

"We will be fine. You go off and enjoy yourself, let your hair down, paint the town red!" I told him. James grinned.

"I think you need to learn some more up-to-date expressions. I shouldn't be more than a couple of hours," he replied.

James left without much fuss. I wandered into the kitchen and put the kettle on.

"Anyone want some cake?" I shouted through to the living room, placing four pieces onto small side plates and carrying them through with me.

As we sat down and began to tuck in to the Victoria sponge in front of the fire, I didn't think again about where exactly he could have gone and who he could have gone with.

I wouldn't think about it again until a few hours later, when the children were tucked in, sleeping soundly in their beds. When a policeman came to the door and asked to come in.

Then everything in our lives would change.

Chapter Forty Eight

Edd

After receiving James's call that morning, I cancelled all of my plans and headed straight over to his house. It didn't take long, as I was already in Kendal, pouring through yet more lists of people Emma knew. I was staggered at the amount of people that it contained and could see why people chose to live anonymously in big cities - where they could get away with murder.

Was I shocked to hear that a note had been put through the door to James's house while he had been out dropping off the children at school?

Both yes and no. I have seen what guilt can do to people. It eats away at them. It niggles in the most unsuspecting moments. After a while, the guilt can become too much. People can just snap. They can just walk into a police station and turn themselves in. As simple as that. Or that piece of evidence that had been vital in securing a conviction suddenly turned up without any warning, in a place that had been frequently searched before. It was enough for them to be reprimanded in custody. It was enough for them to be sent down. It happened more often than you would think.

James and I had discussed many things that afternoon. Who the person could be and what they might know. We hypothesised on whether they were male or female, on whether they would come alone.

I told James about the importance of asking open ended questions. We couldn't be seen to be swaying anyone in one direction or another. We couldn't put words into their mouth. We wanted to dig deeper. We wanted them to admit to things openly. If we were going to use this information to our benefit, we had to be very careful.

We wandered together out to the stepping-stones to have a look around. They were located just opposite a guesthouse with a stone wall marking its boundary; about five-minute' walk from James's house towards Rydal Lake. On the other side of the stepping-stones were open fields that eventually led to the cricket club. The road that we followed from James's house leading up to them was narrow and twisted. We talked about the practicalities as we walked back to the house, and sat at the dining room table, coming up with a plan.

"It's likely that you might know who this person is. It's important that you remain cool and calm," I told James. "You need to put your phone on voice record. Try not to fiddle with it, because you don't want them to become suspicious. You don't want to make them angry. They could be capable of lashing out at you in a split second. You need protection. I've got a couple of guns; Sarah is bringing them down here right away. I'll show you how to load them. If you have to shoot, then go for the legs. It will cause them enough pain to keel over and they won't be able to run after you. I'll get there a couple of hours before, I've made a room reservation at the guesthouse that overlooks the river. I'll watch for any strange movements, any sign that this person isn't working alone. When it starts to get dark, I'll position myself behind the wall. They won't be able to see me clearly, but I should be able to see them. If anything bad happens and things suddenly deteriorate, you get behind that wall as quickly as you can. You must stay alert and vigilant at all times. This could be a trap and the situation could turn sour quite quickly. Whoever killed Emma...well, they might want you too."

James nodded at me, trying to keep up with all of the information that I was telling him. While we took a ten minute break, he called his mother-in-law, Mary, and asked her to come and look after the children. I told him to make sure that the door was locked after him and that I would have someone watching the house while he was gone. We couldn't leave any detail overlooked. What if this was a ploy to get James out of the house? For someone to waltz in and take the children?

Sarah appeared with the guns. I took them and asked her to go back to Mary and Bobs. I couldn't be worrying about her safety too. I knew that Bob would look after her. I then showed James how to use the gun, hoping, all the time, that it would be unnecessary. We talked about how they would be when he found them. They might have had a drink or two for Dutch courage. They might have cycled, or walked even. They might have come in a car so that they could get away more quickly afterwards.

"James, the most important thing you need to remember is that whoever this person is, they could be very dangerous. You need to remain focused. You need to think about the children. Don't do anything that you might later come to regret – no matter what they tell you, or how angry what they say might make you. Whoever this is, they have been watching you. They know your movements. They know what makes you tick. Don't give them the satisfaction of giving in. You can't afford to be put away for a simple mistake. Your children need you. Who will they have if you're in a prison cell for the next twenty years? If the information is important, then we will get whoever has done this. We will get them and then justice will be sought."

James seemed subdued. I could tell that there were so many thoughts going through his mind. So many things to contemplate. At just before three o'clock, I said goodbye. I climbed into my car and drove the short distance to the guesthouse.

I checked in.

I took my bags upstairs to the front bedroom.

I waited.

Chapter Forty Nine

James

  As I left the house that evening, with my torch lighting the way and a gun tucked firmly into my jacket pocket, I felt a strange sense of calm wash over me. I hoped that, for the first time in months, I might go to sleep with more answers than questions. I hoped that whoever had sent the note had known something more than we did, that they held the piece of information that we needed to find our closure.
  I walked slowly along the Under Loughrigg road that evening, down towards the stepping-stones. I tried not to think about the times that Emma and I had brought the children down here for a paddle or a play afterschool. Sometimes, we even crossed the river and had a little picnic tea on the other side.
  As the road began to straighten, I glanced casually around. I couldn't see anyone. I knew that Edd would be hiding somewhere in front of me to my left. I stepped onto the stone and looked out at the river. It was slightly higher than usual, with all the rain we had been having recently, but the stepping-stones were still crossable. I'd seen them buried under a foot of water when the flooding had been bad.

I started stepping across, slowly. When I reached the middle, I stopped. I closed my eyes for a moment and listened to the sound of the flowing water. As I opened them again, I saw the outline of a small, dark figure walking across the field directly ahead of me. I carried on stepping until I reached the other side. The figure became larger and larger as it drew closer to me. I realised quite quickly that the figure belonged to a man, of medium build and around the same height as me. He seemed to be alone, though I remembered Edd's words of warning: Assume nothing. Don't let your guard down.

The man stopped next to me. I studied his face. Did this man look like a killer? Certainly not. Did he look like he had known something about Emma's accident? He seemed to think so, although I wasn't so sure. On closer inspection, this man looked weak and nervous. There was also something slightly familiar about him. I wondered if I had seen him at Emma's funeral, but I couldn't place him at the Kingdom Hall on that day.

Suddenly, something in my mind clicked. I hadn't seen him at all at Emma's funeral. He hadn't been at the Kingdom Hall to say his goodbyes to Emma. But he had been at another event. The man in front of me had been a guest at my wedding. Yet, still, I could not remember his name. John? Albert? As I was thinking, he began to speak.

"James. I haven't seen you for a long time." He looked at my face, studied my clothing. He seemed to be enjoying the fact that I couldn't place him. That I couldn't put a name to his face.

"Fred Jones," he said. I frowned. Something about Jones seemed familiar. Then the penny dropped. I knew who this man was. But why on earth would he know something about who had harmed Emma? Even more confusing, still, why would he – a Witness, of all people - have wanted to harm my wife?

"You came to our wedding," I said. It was more of a statement than a question.

"We did, yes. Seems like so long ago now, doesn't it? A day when each of us had our loving wives by our side." I didn't respond.

"I've come here, James, to tell you the truth. I've come here because unlike them, I believe in good things. I don't believe in keeping secrets. I don't believe that your children should grow up without knowing what happened to their mother. But it's going to take some time. There are many things that came before that day, you see. The day of the accident. I know that once I've finished, you will want to call the police. I'm ready, James. I'm ready to pay for my crimes. I cannot live like this anymore."

I nodded at him, and sat down on a large stone. I could see the outline of Edd's shadow over the wall. We had agreed on a signal. If I raised my right hand and started to itch my head, he would call the police immediately.

I knew, in that moment, exactly who Fred Jones was. I knew exactly how he slotted into Emma's life. What I couldn't believe was, that after suffering the loss of his own wife, that Fred had seemed it right to destroy more families. It just didn't make sense.

"It started long before we even knew you, long before your wedding. Erica and Emma were good friends. After Emma had moved back up north and had Poppy. Emma and Erica would go out together on their ministry work. They would take the children to the Kingdom Hall on a Sunday morning. Emma and I had met at work, and at that time, I didn't know that she was a Witness. To me, she was just a normal, beautiful woman.

"You can't stop loving someone on the basis of their religious beliefs. I wasn't a Witness, never have been. I didn't mind it as such, it just wasn't for me. I'd had a tough life as a kid and I just couldn't accept that an all-loving God would allow so many bad things to happen to good people. So Erica and I married at the local registry office, had the two boys. Life was good. But then Erica started to get sick. She had a couple of operations in Halifax that were not without risk. Bloodless surgeries. It turned out, in the end, that the only thing that would save her was a blood transfusion. We started to fight about it, about what she should do. Life at home was becoming difficult for the boys. It wasn't good for them to see us fighting all the time - it wasn't right.

"You and Emma got married at the beginning of Erica's illness. By the time Emma was pregnant with Finn, Erica had deteriorated at an alarming rate. They went together to an assembly about Jehovah's Will. I know that they talked about Erica's predicament. I know that she listened to

Emma. Then, one night, we had the absolute mother of all arguments. I told Erica that she was being selfish. She told me that she had already decided and that was it. So I got a lawyer, and I prepared to take my wife to court. Do you know how bad that made me feel? Do you know what it felt like, knowing that I was going against her religion? I understood why she didn't want the blood, but it just didn't seem logical. Erica was prepared to die; she was prepared to leave behind our two small boys. For what? *Eternal salvation*, that's what she said. It was a load of codswallop, in my mind.

"Anyway, in the end, I was too late. Erica died two days before the court hearing. Sometimes, I like to believe that the court hearing would have saved her life, but really – I'm not convinced. We live in an age where people are allowed to have their own opinions. We live in an age where people have choices. Erica's choice was to die. Nothing I said or did would have mattered."

Fred stopped talking for a moment, as if he were collecting his thoughts. I remembered Erica from our wedding. I knew that she and Emma had once been close friends. I knew that Mary believed that Erica's death had been the main factor in Emma leaving her medical documents in her bedside table. We would never know, now though, for sure.

"Erica's funeral was at the Kingdom Hall. I didn't want to have it there, but what choice did I have? Her parents had been Witnesses for all of their lives. They were not going to let her have a normal funeral. It felt like the final stab in the back, that day. All of these people, strangers to me, telling me how Erica was happy now, and at peace. All of these people having the last laugh, because they had brainwashed Erica into her beliefs. She was dead because of them. She could have lived for years, you know. She could have watched our boys grow. What did our sons have now? Nothing. It felt wrong; it was just so wrong...In those early days, after I had lost Erica, I couldn't function. I was angry at the world, angry with Jehovah Witnesses. But do you know who else I was angry at? Emma. Emma and Erica had been good friends. Emma was a mother herself; she should have known the importance of being there for her children. She should never have encouraged Erica not to have the transfusions. If anyone could have made a difference, it was Emma. But she let Erica down. She encouraged her faith. Emma didn't even come to Erica's funeral. I mean, what kind of a friend is that?"

I thought, for a moment, about Emma and Erica. I knew that they had become distant when Erica's illness had really started to take hold. We had just had Finn. Life with a new baby was chaotic – the sleepless night, the never-ending cycle of feeding and changing. Was what Fred was saying really true? I was beginning to wonder how it all began to fit together, when Fred started to talk again.

"A year after Erica had gone, I was still angry. Angry and depressed. But I had my boys and they were helping me through the difficult times. We didn't go anywhere near the Kingdom Hall anymore. Erica's Mum and Dad were upset. They started making calls. Children's Services started appearing on my doorstep. They started complaining about how often the children had arrived late for school, about how Charlie had a grazed knee. They appeared a couple of evenings when the boys were in bed. I didn't touch a drop before then, you must know that. But I'd had a few beers. I gave them a piece of my mind. Before I knew it, I was being dragged to court. They said that I was 'incapable' of looking after them. That the boys would be better off going to live with Erica's parents. So that's what happened. Access for me was one night a week and on a Saturday afternoon. I couldn't even have my boys overnight at my house. Do you know how that made me feel? They had already lost their mother. There was no need for this. No need at all.

So, for another couple of years, I plodded on. I tried hard to be a good parent. I tried to do all the right things, tick all of the right boxes. I stopped drinking, I worked longer hours, and I bought a bigger house, which I kept clean and tidy. But the people who had taken my boys away didn't want to know about it. They wouldn't give me five minutes of their time. So that's when I started thinking about Emma. I thought that she was the one person who might help me to get the boys back.

But Emma didn't want to know. She told me that she couldn't get involved. So I started to follow her. I didn't mean to hurt her, James. I didn't mean that. I just wanted my boys back. I just needed help. I followed her around a bit. One day, I followed her to Morecambe, where she met a woman who I didn't recognise. That's when it started to go bad. After Emma had left, I followed this other woman. I wanted to talk to her, to find out what they had been talking about, but she wouldn't tell me anything. So I stuck around. I had a beer. That's when I did it. I knocked her over. I didn't mean to, you know. I just meant to put the wind up her a bit. But when I got out of my car, she looked bad. She had no pulse. So I just drove off."

"You killed Jean Witton?" I asked him, in disbelief. He nodded. "Didn't you know that she has a husband and a young son? You thought that Emma and Jean were up to something? Didn't you know that Emma had a baby who died? Jean had been in the hospital at the same time..."

"I didn't know. But I did later. I did feel bad, but I wouldn't turn myself in, how could I? I was trying to get my boys back. Admitting that I had run over a woman in cold blood? I would only ever see my boys again through tainted glass."

I raised my arm and scratched my head. Fred was looking at me; I saw the light flicker on Edd's phone. I hoped that the police wouldn't take long.

"So what did you do to Emma?" I felt sick. This man had problems, that much was clear.

"I tried to call her, to talk to her. All I ever got was her voicemail. So I kept on following her. I started to notice patterns in her behaviour. I knew that on Sunday evenings, she went out to see her friend as regular as clockwork. I watched her go that Sunday. I got some beers in my car. I pulled up on the side of the road, just after the turn off over the bridge, which was on Emma's route home. I waited for her to come back. I saw her figure moving closer to me. I was getting ready to get out of my car, have a little word with her. That's when it happened. Emma was walking over the bridge when a car was coming the other way too fast; she was just about to turn when it hit her, head on."

I was trying to take it all in. Was Fred really telling the truth? How could I be sure?

"The lads in the car, just young lads, stopped. I took down their car's registration number. Emma wasn't in a good way. They argued about what they should do, but it was clear to me that they had been drinking. Who was I to jump out and give them the riot act? I had done exactly the same thing, after all."

"You didn't kill Emma?"

"No... but what I did was far worse. All this time I could have told you. All this time you could have had closure..."

"You know that after Erica was gone, Emma's medical documents remained in her bedside table. But she never removed the codicil. The trauma to her brain was too much; she was never going to come out of that accident well..."

Fred and I surveyed each other. I could hear the faint sirens of police cars coming from both directions.

"Fred, we have both lost someone very special to us. We have both suffered more than we needed to, for many different reasons. We now have to do what is right. You're going to have to tell the police about Jean Witton. I've met her husband. He's a sound bloke. He doesn't deserve to live the rest of his life not knowing the truth."

Fred nodded. I could see that he was starting to cry. That all of this had been a lot for him to do; it had compromised everything that he had tried to accomplish for his children.

"The other thing, Fred. That registration number. You're going to have to give it to the police. They have to know. These people, they can't do things like that and just get away with it...it isn't right..."

The sirens began moving closer.

"I'll never see my lads again, will I?" he asked me.

"People make mistakes, Fred. Sometimes they are big, sometimes small. You've kept things hidden from the police; I know that much is true. But you know what your main mistake in this has been?" I asked him. He shook his head.

"Loving your family," I said.

"What's done is done. But from now on, you need to think about those boys. I'll do what I can to help you. But Erica's parents aren't as bad as you think. They'll take care of them. They will grow up into wonderful men. You just have to believe."

The police pulled up their cars on the opposite side of the river.

We walked back across, just as Edd came out from his hiding place.

The policeman read Fred his rights, and placed him in handcuffs.

"Go easy on him," Edd told him, gently.

"Do you need us to come to the station?" I asked the officer.

"We'll call if we need you. You can get yourselves home."

Edd nodded to me, as I had one last look at Fred being bundled into the back of the police car. He was in for a long night.

We walked away from the river, neither of us daring to speak. As we entered the house, Mary sprang to her feet. A police officer was sat next to her on the sofa.

"What on earth is going on?! You two have got some explaining to do!"

Chapter Fifty

Edd

The next few days were a frenzy of activity. I managed to retreat to Cumwhinton to avoid the worst of the press. Before I had left, I had helped James to prepare a small statement to read out to the national newspapers, and I hoped that would be enough to keep the reporters from hounding on his doorstep and asking insensitive questions.

With Fred Jones in custody, the local police immediately set to tracing the make and model of the car that had knocked Emma down that night. It took them less than a day to reprimand four young boys, aged between eighteen and twenty-one. One by one, their stories fell apart. They admitted to their crimes, and were now awaiting trial at Carlisle Crown Court in a few days time. The driver, of course, faced the worst charges – death by dangerous driving, and driving under the influence of alcohol, and it seemed likely that the others would be charged with perverting the course of justice.

Was I relieved that it was all over? Of course I was. Though I was slightly irritated that the police had been right with their assumptions. I felt, though, that I had put Emma's family firmly on the road to recovery. I had helped them to lay to rest many of their troubles. Sophie was already building new relationships with her biological family. James was getting there, slowly. Roy Witton could now move on from his wife's death with a more clear focus. Jean hadn't been murdered in cold blood; her death was entirely preventable. It seemed sad to lose a woman who felt able to speak the truth. Roy would receive a payout, which would allow him to live a more comfortable life, but money isn't always everything. I was sure that he would have his wife back in a heartbeat if it were at all possible.

I enjoyed taking some time out in the few days leading up to the trial. Sarah and I enjoyed some lazy mornings together at the house. I popped round to see Alan, went into Carlisle to do a bit of shopping. Every evening I called Bob and Mary, just after six o clock. They were getting there. Mary was a woman who could forgive. I wasn't entirely sure how, but she seemed to find peace with the truth. It seemed to have allowed her to close a door and open a window. Mary and Bob knew Fred's mother-in-law from the Kingdom Hall fairly well. They had called round to see her the day after he had been reprimanded. She bought the children sweets and told them that their father was a very brave and noble man. Mary believed that there had already been too much pain, too many lives lost. Fred was getting the help he needed now - the psychiatric help and the medication. One day, he too would be free from grief and pain. One day, he would be free to love and look after his family.

As I pulled out my suit, ready for Sarah to iron, ready for the trial tomorrow, I thought about all of the moments that made it happen. The murder of Elizabeth, the adoption of Emma and Sophie, baby Iris, having faith. But what was at the centre of all of those things? Losing someone you love. Being able to accept that what's done is done, and being able to move on with dignity.

I sincerely hoped that for Mary and Bob, Sophie, James and the children, tomorrow would be the first day of the rest of their lives. Of understanding and acceptance. Life may not have turned out how they had wanted. It may still be tainted with such pain and sorrow of losing Emma before her time. But one day, they will be able to look back at the good times they had shared, at the things that had brought them together. I had no doubt that if eternal salvation really existed, then Jean Witton, Erica Jones, and Emma Parker would be there, waiting to live with all of those that they loved most, in paradise earth.

Chapter Fifty One

Mary

The trial lasted for several days. I didn't go to every session; I just couldn't. I didn't want to hear the gruesome details of the accident. I couldn't listen to the report of a traffic officer who had stopped the driver the day after and breathalysed him. He was still well over the legal limit. But he got away with no more than a slap on the wrist – they hadn't asked him where he had been the night before, if he had driven home. If they had, they would have known for sure. That they had been driving round in a car with so much alcohol in their system that it's a wonder that they had only managed to knock down and kill one woman. It really was shocking.

As we sat together, waiting for the verdict that would give us peace, I thought about how Emma had been as a little girl. One day, I'd taken the girls strawberry picking. The sun was hot and the girls ran around the fields in their cotton dresses. Sophie and Emma decided that they'd had enough. They walked over to the farmer's barn and fell asleep in the hay. I have the photo somewhere at home – their rosy red cheeks, the glorious sunshine. I thought of other times, the day that Bob had taught her to ride a bike. Her first day at secondary school.

How strong she had been to leave Joe and come home to us, pregnant and alone.

We could sit around and mope. We could think about how life was cruel and how Emma should be here with us at every special moment. Or we could let it go. We could remember what Emma had been when she was with us, but not dwell that she was no longer here. We could make something good happen out of something bad, if we tried hard enough. I strongly believed that we owed it to Emma to try.

I looked around the courtroom as the judge began with the formalities. We sat together in the public gallery – Bob and I, Sophie, James, Hannah, and Edd. We were hoping for a verdict that would allow those responsible to reflect on their actions and change. We had seen a heartbreaking video of Poppy and Finn, talking about Emma. Our solicitor was confident. Yet, still, I held my breath as the verdict was read aloud.

"And do you find the defendant guilty, or not guilty?" the judge asked the jury.

You could have heard a pin drop in that moment. You could have heard the sound of a butterfly flapping its wings.

"Guilty."

*

Outside the courtroom, the mood was euphoric. James made a short statement to the newspaper crew who had been firmly camped outside all week. As I looked across the road, I saw three white pigeons sat high in the only tree for miles around. I smiled.

We found a little bar on a side street, and Bob ordered a bottle of champagne. Glasses clinked. It was over. As people started to leave, I wandered over to have a word with James.

"I'm glad it's all over, Mary," he said to me.

"Things will start to get easier soon; I really do believe it." I replied. James looked around the room with a puzzled expression.

"Where's Hannah gone?" he asked.

"She went home. I expect that she has a lot on her mind..." I told him, without elaborating. James frowned.

"She should be here, with the rest of us. Celebrating...for Emma."

"James, sometimes even in the worst of times, there are people worse off than you." I told him, softly.

"I don't understand what you mean?"

"Hannah has a lot going on in her life at the moment... you know, personally."

I let that thought hang in the air for a moment before putting James out of his misery.

"Look, I don't know this for sure; I could be way off the mark...but we'll call it female intuition..."

"Call what?"

"The pale face, the tiredness, the sickness in the mornings..."

James's face suddenly dropped; his mouth fell open.

"I do believe, James, that Hannah is pregnant."

Chapter Fifty Two

<u>James</u>

Struggling to hide my shock from Mary, I excused myself to go to the toilet. I closed the cubical door and sat, silently, wondering.

Could Hannah really be pregnant? Was I an absolute idiot for realising this now, months later? That pregnancy could be something that we would have to think about? Of course I was.

Emma had been sterilised after Millie, so it wasn't something that had been at the forefront of my mind for some time. We had sat down and had a reasonable, grown up conversation about it. Three children were enough. We didn't have the time, or the energy for another, and we didn't want to have to invest in a people carrier just to be able to ship our family from a to b. Emma hadn't been keen on carrying on taking the pill as a long-term solution. If she didn't have menopause until she was fifty, there was potentially another fifteen years of her being fertile. The snip terrified me – I knew that other men had done it, but I would rather not. I know what you're thinking - I was there when Emma gave birth to two of our children. But I just couldn't do it. I couldn't even make an appointment to talk about it without crossing my legs. But Hannah's fertility? Clearly, that was a completely different situation.

What if Mary was right? How could we manage with four children? Yet what if she was wrong? What if the baby wasn't mine? I stamped down that thought as soon as I'd had it. I could be a real idiot when I wanted to be. Hannah wasn't like that. If Hannah was pregnant, there could only be one father, and I was looking right at him. If Hannah really was pregnant, then I was going to have to man up and I was going to have to do it quickly. Hannah needed my help now, more than ever. Hannah needed to know that she wasn't on her own. That it didn't have to be like this. That we shouldn't be living as if we were strangers.

As I drove home, I had a million different thoughts running through my head. It was funny, how a good mood can suddenly come crashing down. Why hadn't I noticed? That much was plainly obvious, even to me. Since the day we had let go of Emma, I had shut Hannah out completely. I tried hard not to look at her for more than a few seconds. Tried not to raise anyone's suspicions. I had tried to forget about that night. I thought that her tiredness was surely just the same as mine – that the guilt of what we had done had ebbed away at her; that when the rest of the world was sleeping, she thought about Emma too.

I parked the car by the chip shop and wandered down Vicarage Road to collect the children from the private day nursery. Millie came out with various finger paintings, Finn some kind of cardboard robot, and Poppy with some kind of pasta necklace. I chatted briefly to the nursery staff, who, of course, had already heard the verdict. They were probably wondering why I didn't seem as happy as I ought to be right now, but there was nothing else that I could really say. Justice had been sought, but Emma was still gone. And I, her husband, had seemingly managed to impregnate another woman while she had still been alive. I shuddered to think about the gossip that would soon be circling the village.

We arrived back home without too much fuss. The children went into the living room to play with their toys, while I went to the kitchen to start preparing something for dinner. *What was I going to say to Hannah?* I wondered. Was she ever planning to tell me, or was she going to wait until her ever-expanding bulge gave it all away? Did she really think that I wouldn't notice when she turned up with a baby?

As I served out plates of pasta and cheese to the children, I realised that I was going to have to speak to her, face to face, as soon as possible. That I wouldn't be able to sleep at all without knowing the truth.

"Okay kids; hurry up. No time for a bath tonight. I'm going to call Hannah and see if she can come over for a while, so you'll have to be on your best behaviour. Stories and then straight to bed."

"You can't do that Daddy," Poppy said. I glanced across at her.

"No Daddy, Auntie Hanny is too busy to see us for some times," Finn added, continuing to eat his pasta.

It amazed me that she had offered the children an explanation to her absence in our lives, that she had even thought about how her not being here as often would affect the children.

"Well, how about I'll call her and see?" I asked them. Finn shook his head.

"Daddy, you're not listening to us. Hannah won't be able to come and see us today, because Hannah is going to live in Mexico!" Poppy said excitedly.

"Mexico?!" I managed to utter.

"She's going tonight," Finn added.

I didn't need another second to make my decision.

"Right, coats on, wellies on. We're going to find Hannah, and were going right now!"

Chapter Fifty Three

<u>Hannah</u>

I came straight home from Preston as soon as I could. I could feel Mary's eyes rest on me, for a moment more than was really needed, as I told her that I was tired and I wanted to go home and rest. I was far too emotional to be dealing with this; I didn't trust myself not to say something that I would later regret.

As I glanced across the room, I saw James, who was chatting happily to someone I didn't recognise. I needed to go home, and finish packing my bags. In a few hours, I had a plane to catch. A new life awaited me. I had to be prepared.

The journey home was uneventful. The M6 was moving freely, which was a miracle in itself. When I got home, I wandered around the house and packed the last few things that needed to go in my suitcase.

Was I making the right choice? Who knows? But what I did know was that being here didn't help. Everywhere I went, I saw Emma. Every shop, every corner. There were so many memories that I had of her that it was impossible to erase them all. Impossible that she wouldn't come back to me when I was sitting by my desk at work, or standing in the queue in the spar. I needed space. I needed to figure out where my life was going and how it was all going to work. I couldn't do that here. There were too many people that I knew, too many people that I felt I had to justify my life to. You can't live like that. You have to make your own choices and live with the consequences. You can't just live how everyone else thinks you should.

Was I worried about what lay ahead? I was terrified.

I knew that I was taking the easy way out. Taking a sabbatical from work so soon after losing Emma didn't prompt any unnecessary questions. My boss had signed my request form and told me to go and enjoy myself. The reality was that a few months in Mexico weren't going to make my life any easier. I knew, in my heart of hearts, that I should talk to James; at least, tell him the truth. Surely, I owed him that much. But what was the point? What could he do about it now? The damage had already been done. I had already made up my mind, alone, with a bottle of white wine, a few weeks ago. I wasn't getting any younger. I wasn't in a stable relationship. What if this was it - my only chance to have a child?

James had enough to worry about. Adding to his burdens wasn't going to help anything. Besides, he had already made his position crystal clear. We had been a mistake. That night shouldn't have happened. If that's what he really believed, then telling him the truth wouldn't help. It would only make things a hundred times worse.

The airport taxi was running late. I looked at the clock that hung on the kitchen wall. I went upstairs to double-check that I hadn't left anything behind – phone chargers and my toothbrush. I checked that I had my passport and my plane tickets in my hand luggage. I made sure I'd left a note for my next-door neighbour, who had kindly agreed to pop in every day and feed the cat while I was gone. I suspected she might not be so hospitable towards me when she realised the truth upon my return. Very soon, I was going to be public enemy number one.

As the doorbell rang, I breathed a sigh of relief, and heaved my heavy suitcase behind me. But when I opened the door, ready to offer the man my suitcase, I found James looking up at me.

"James?" I said to him, wondering what on earth he was doing on my doorstep at this time of the night.

"Hannah," he replied.

I looked behind him to see that he had landed his car badly in a parking bay. That the three children were grinning and waving at me from the back seat.

"This isn't really a good time...." I began.

"Poppy and Finn told me you were going to Mexico?" he asked, perplexed.

"That's right." What else could I say? This wasn't the time or the place. I just wanted to slip away, quietly, without a scene.

"Hannah, look. I know I've been an idiot. I know that I shouldn't have shut you out like I did. But running away from your problems isn't going to help. I don't want you to be a stranger to me. It's all been a bit much, you know, on top of everything else. I can't think straight. I don't want to go upsetting other people. I don't want people to think that I can just...move on. To think that Emma wasn't important to me. Because I can't – things just aren't that simple. I think about Emma all the time. But I also know that, well, I know that we could make things work, couldn't we?" he said, looking at me, pleadingly.

"Look...James...it's really not that simple."

"It's not?" he asked, surprised.

The airport taxi pulled into the space next to where James had left the car. He began opening the boot to make room for my things.

"James...I'm..."

"I know, Mary told me," he said, flatly.

"Mary?" I asked, my face, no doubt, showing the disbelief that I felt. How had Mary known?

"Women's intuition, apparently," James replied, as if sensing my thoughts.

"I know it's not...ideal...I know that the timing couldn't be worse. I hardly know what I'm going to do about it myself, really. But I don't want you to feel pressured. I don't want you to feel obligated. That isn't fair. It isn't what you want."

"But what if it is what I want? Are you saying that you're not even going to give us a chance?" he asked me.

"I'm saying that, for now, we all need space. Three months isn't long, James. Not in the grand scheme of things. I'll be back. I promise."

He looked at me, cautiously.

"And when you are back? Will it be for good?"

"I wish I knew. But I do know that I won't shut you out, James. That you can be who you want to be for this baby, if that's what you want. But look, those three children need you. You need to go and look after your family."

We glanced at the children sitting in the car as the airport taxi man took my suitcase. James placed a hand on my lower stomach. He looked me straight in the eye.

"But I won't be able to look after all of my family. Not until you come back to us. We need you. Please Hannah. Don't go. Not now."

"James, I have to. This is for the best..."

I climbed into the taxi and clipped my belt. I felt like I was letting go of everyone I cared about. I felt like I was letting Emma down, that I wasn't doing the right thing for her children. As the taxi pulled out onto the road, I managed to wave goodbye.

Emma would have wanted me to live life to the full. She would have wanted the children to be carefree, wanted James to move on. We all needed space, and time to heal.

Letting go of Emma was the hardest thing that we had ever had to do.

Anything after that would be easy.

Epilogue: One Year Later

James

Fourteen months have passed since my wife was knocked down one night on the way home.

It's been one year now since that awful day in which we let Emma go.

Ten months since the driver who was responsible for her death was sentenced to twenty-five years in prison.

It's been seven months since Hannah came back from Mexico.

Five months since we moved into a larger house that would fit in all of our expanding family.

Three months since she gave us the gift that we now call Barney, the happy little bundle of life who had been conceived in a moment of sadness.

It's been two months since we were married at the registry office in Kendal.

What has all of this taught us? That life moves in mysterious ways.

Not a day goes by that we don't think about Emma. That we don't hear her laughter, or see her smile. Not a day goes by that a memory of her comes back to us, in the most unsuspecting moments.

For three hundred and sixty-five days, we have wished that Emma was still here - but she is not. For every day that Emma is not with us, we try to live our lives just as she would have wanted, even though it isn't always easy.

We are happy and carefree.

We help others.

We make small acts of kindness to those who we think need help.

And the most important thing of all?

We can forgive.

THE END

About the Author

Brooke is a mother, hen keeper, qualified teacher, PA, and private tutor.

In her spare time you will usually find her swimming in a lake or riding over a mountain on her bike. She drinks a lot of tea, likes books, and loves cake.

Brooke lives in the Lake District with her family.

Her first novel, *"The Missing Half"* was published in August 2013. This is her second novel.

To find out more visit:

www.brookepowley.com